"We have a real mystery on our hands."

Carrie's gray-blue eyes sparkled with mischief. She lowered her voice to a melodramatic whisper. "Who is the wealthy but anonymous Frenchman, and why is he interested in Jack Harrington? And why is he terrorizing Carrie Bishop, an unsuspecting tourist from Des Moines who has unwittingly gotten herself caught up in a web of trickery and deceit—"

"Carrie, stop that!" Jack cut in. "This is not exciting, and we are not television detectives. This is *my* mystery, not ours. I don't want to be responsible for involving you in something when I don't have the faintest notion of what it's all about. Now if this creep comes near you again, scream as loud as you can for the nearest cop. Got that?"

The amusement left Carrie's face. "You mean I really *could* be in danger?" she whispered.

Dear Reader:

Happy holidays! Our authors join me in wishing you all the best for a joyful, loving holiday season with your family and friends. And while celebrating the new year—and the new decade!—I hope you'll think of Silhouette Books.

1990 promises to be especially happy here. This year marks our tenth anniversary, and we're planning a celebration! To symbolize the timelessness of love, as well as the modern gift of the tenth anniversary, each month in 1990, we're presenting readers with a *Diamond Jubilee* Silhouette Romance title, penned by one of your all-time favorite Silhouette Romance authors.

In January, under the Silhouette Romance line's *Diamond Jubilee* emblem, look for Diana Palmer's next book in her bestselling LONG, TALL TEXANS series—*Ethan*. He's a hero sure to lasso your heart! And just in time for Valentine's Day, Brittany Young has written *The Ambassador's Daughter*. Spend the most romantic month of the year in France, the setting for this magical classic. Victoria Glenn, Annette Broadrick, Peggy Webb, Dixie Browning, Phyllis Halldorson—to name just a few!—have written *Diamond Jubilee* titles especially for you. And Pepper Adams has penned a trilogy about three very rugged heroes—and their lovely heroines!—set on the plains of Oklahoma. Look for the first book this summer.

The *Diamond Jubilee* celebration is Silhouette Romance's way of saying thanks to you, our readers. We've been together for ten years now, and with the support you've given us, you can look forward to many more years of heartwarming, poignant love stories.

I hope you'll enjoy this book and all of the stories to come. Come home to romance—Silhouette Romance—for always!

Sincerely,

Tara Hughes Gavin
Senior Editor

KAREN LEABO

Ten Days in Paradise

Silhouette Romance

Published by Silhouette Books New York

America's Publisher of Contemporary Romance

SILHOUETTE BOOKS
300 E. 42nd St., New York, N.Y. 10017

ISBN: 0-373-08692-X

First Silhouette Books printing December 1989

Printed in the U.S.A.

Books by Karen Leabo

Silhouette Romance

Roses Have Thorns #648
Ten Days in Paradise #692

KAREN LEABO

credits her fourth-grade teacher for initially sparking her interest in creative writing. She was determined at an early age to have her work published. When she was in the eighth grade she wrote a children's book and convinced her school yearbook publisher to put it in print.

Karen was born and raised in Dallas, Texas, but now lives in a Victorian house that overlooks the Kansas City, Missouri, skyline. When she's not writing fiction, she's editing newsletters and writing business plans for a venture-capital company.

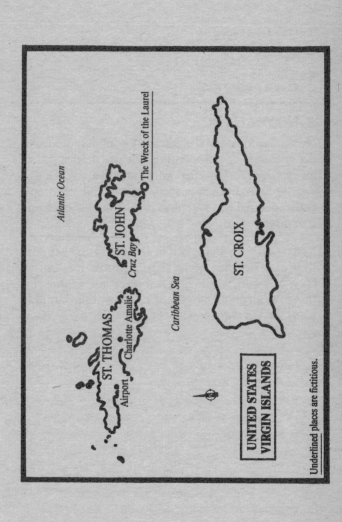

Atlantic Ocean

The Wreck of the Laurel

ST. JOHN

Cruz Bay

ST. THOMAS

Charlotte Amalie

Airport

Caribbean Sea

ST. CROIX

UNITED STATES
VIRGIN ISLANDS

Underlined places are fictitious.

Chapter One

The first thing Jack Harrington saw when he surfaced was a pair of legs—not ordinary legs, but spectacular, peaches-and-cream female legs. They were dangling over the edge of the pier, and he indulged himself in blatant appreciation for the span of about five seconds. But after removing his mask and snorkel, he got a better look at the slender blond woman to whom the legs were attached, and appreciation turned into raw fury. She was taking pictures of *his* boat.

The fact that she was snooping around looked fishy enough on its own merit. But her activities were doubly suspect because of what Jack had just discovered *under* his boat. He intended to find out what was going on.

The woman wasn't yet aware of his presence. Jack inched closer to her, moving noiselessly through the water, then with a quick movement he encircled her slim ankle with his hand.

She shrieked, and the pocket camera flew out of her hands and into the water. "What are you *doing* down there?" she cried.

"I'm the one who should be asking the questions," Jack responded smoothly. "What are *you* doing here, taking pictures of my boat?"

"Since when did photography become illegal?" the woman shot back defensively. She tried to sound angry, but Jack knew the signs of pure fear when he saw them. Her pale gray-blue eyes were wide with fright, and the pulse at her ankle, where Jack's thumb was pressing, raced out of control. He felt a momentary pang of remorse, and he wondered briefly what it would be like to feel her pulse race for another reason altogether. Instantly he clamped down on that line of thinking. Such thoughts could get him into trouble.

"Photography becomes illegal when you use it for sabotage. What were you doing, getting a good look at my sonar equipment so your friends can figure out how to mess it up? Looking for where I keep my maps, maybe?"

The woman appeared genuinely puzzled, and her voice took on an edge of hysteria. "I have no earthly idea what you're talking about, and if you don't let go of my ankle—"

"And I suppose you don't know anything about this, right?" He pulled his other hand out of the water to reveal a strange-looking hand tool. Minutes ago, he'd picked it up off the sandy ocean floor directly under his boat.

"I don't even know what that is!"

"It's a manual drill with an auger bit, and it was used to eat a three-inch hole in the hull of my boat. And if you don't know anything about that, then why don't you just explain what you're doing here?"

Suddenly the woman looked as if she'd had enough. Her eyes narrowed, and her hands balled up into fists. She spoke through clenched teeth. "I'm *here* for the hotel's one-thirty scuba class. I arrived on St. Thomas last night from Des Moines, Iowa, with absolutely no intention of sabotaging anyone. I was taking pictures of your boat because it happens to have the same name I do. Now is that good enough for you, or do you want to check my driver's license?"

Jack glanced at his boat, then uneasily at the woman. Abruptly he relinquished his hold on her ankle. For God's sake, what was he thinking? From her fair skin to her souvenir Virgin Islands T-shirt to the cheap Instamatic camera she'd dropped in the water, she had Des Moines, Iowa, written all over her. Her story, told in that undeniably midwestern accent, had the ring of truth about it. He *did* have a scuba class scheduled for one-thirty, and he was beginning to feel like an idiot. "Your name's Carrie?"

She nodded, still staring at him through slitted cat's eyes.

"I might have been a little hasty, I guess."

"I'll say," came the reply. Her voice was still a bit shaky. "And what about my camera? When you startled me I dropped it into the water. I don't suppose you intend to replace it?"

"Maybe I won't have to. Hold on." He set the drill—his only piece of evidence—on the edge of the pier. Then he pulled on his mask and sank into the crystal-clear water. He kicked his flippered feet a couple of times, and in a matter of seconds had located the camera resting in some seaweed. When he surfaced again, holding the camera aloft triumphantly, Carrie hardly looked mollified.

"It can't possibly still work."

"I've seen them survive saltwater dunkings before," Jack said. "And if it's ruined, I'll buy you another, and I'll throw in a couple of rolls of film. Fair enough?"

She dried the camera with her hotel beach towel and looked it over dubiously. Then she aimed it at Jack and snapped off a shot. The shutter worked, and the film advanced. "Okay," she finally agreed. Quite unexpectedly, she burst out laughing, and the tension between them seemed to disintegrate. "Lord, you scared me to death when you put your cold, wet hand on my ankle like that. Me, underwater sabotage? I can hardly swim at all, much less think about something else while I'm doing it."

Jack found himself smiling in return. He felt ridiculous for having believed this innocent midwestern farm girl could have sabotaged anything. Carrie had the face of an angel, all smooth and rounded and pink from the sun. He was thankful she also had a sense of humor.

Logic dictated that he end the conversation there and leave to make arrangements for repairs to his boat. But something about Carrie—an ingenuousness he seldom encountered, perhaps—prompted him to hang around for a few minutes, at least until the rest of the scuba students showed up and he could tell them the class was canceled.

"So you can barely swim and you signed up for my scuba class?" Jack asked, deftly hoisting himself out of the water and onto the pier beside her.

Her eyes registered faint surprise as she surveyed his dripping body. She scooted a few inches away from him. "Oh, so *you're* Jack Harrington. I suppose I should have figured that out. I signed up for your class because Myra— you know Myra, the hotel tour director?"

Jack nodded.

"She reassured me that scuba diving was easy, even for weak swimmers, and that you were patient with beginners."

He shrugged, not knowing whether to thank Myra later or throttle her for sending him this greenest of water nymphs. "I like to think I'm good at putting my students at ease," he acknowledged. "But I'm afraid there won't be a class today, or tomorrow, or probably for the next week while the *Carrie* is in dry dock, unless I can borrow another boat. Sorry."

For an instant Carrie looked crestfallen, and Jack felt an enormous, out-of-proportion sense of guilt for having disappointed her. But then she was smiling sheepishly. "The truth of the matter, Mr. Harrington, is that the idea of scuba diving scares me, especially in the ocean with sharks and who knows what. I probably wouldn't have gone through with it, and then I would have wasted my money. It's just as well the class got canceled."

Jack quirked his dark eyebrows at her thoughtfully. He always found it difficult to comprehend the fear of water; he'd been swimming like a porpoise since before he could remember.

"You'd like it once you were down there," he said confidently. Much to his surprise, he found himself saying, "I'll have some time on my hands over the next couple of days. We could go to this real calm cove I know of—"

She shook her head. "I don't think so. I thought I wanted to try diving, but . . . Ah, I see the rest of your class is on its way over. I'll leave you to give them the bad news." She jumped to her feet and snatched up her tote bag and towel.

"Wait, don't go yet." But she was already gone, fleeing up the pier and around a family of four headed his way. Apparently they were to have been the rest of his scuba class. Quickly he explained to them about the mishap to his boat. When he'd sent them on their way he scanned the beach for some sign of Carrie. But she had quite thoroughly escaped him, and he hadn't even asked her for a last name. How would he find her in that enormous hotel without a last name?

Then he laughed at himself and shook his head. Why would he want to find her, anyway? He couldn't deny that he found her attractive. She was slender and fair, with honey-blond hair caught up in a ponytail, and an upturned nose that could drive him crazy. Her high, firm breasts, flat stomach and taut but shapely hips had to be the product of an active life. She would have looked beautiful swimming underwater.

Jack shook his head again. Years ago he'd given up wooing tourists, and Carrie didn't seem the type to indulge in a vacation fling. Too conservative. Hell, for all Jack knew she was here with a husband or a gaggle of girlfriends.

He consciously focused his attention on his wounded boat. Damn! He'd worked a lot of years and saved a lot of money in order to purchase the slick little cabin cruiser with its full complement of deep-water diving and light salvage gear. Hadn't had her more than a month, and already this disaster. Obviously someone had been watching him on his recent forays to St. John, and that someone wanted to delay his progress on the *Laurel*.

But who would do that? He thought he'd left all his adversaries in Florida years ago. Why would anyone have the slightest interest in the fact that he was poking around a worthless turn-of-the-century shipwreck that had been picked clean years ago?

A few days' delay wouldn't do him much harm. The sabotage had been more of an intimidation tactic than anything, Jack decided. The finders-keepers philosophy that ruled in the Virgin Islands opened the door for all sorts of illicit activities. It appeared some other people were interested in the *Laurel*, and they were trying to scare Jack away.

Even if they succeeded—and they wouldn't, of course—it wouldn't do them any good. No one but Jack knew exactly where to look . . . or what to look for.

His only clue to the identity of the saboteur was the drill that had been left behind, but it was a weak clue, he reflected. The drill was old, and there was no way to trace it. Unless he had a witness... aha, a witness! Though Carrie was no saboteur, perhaps she'd *seen* something significant while she'd waited on the dock. He hadn't thought to ask her about that.

He could locate her through Myra. Though Myra firmly supported the hotel's strict policy about giving out information on guests, she could nudge Jack in the right direction. She owed him at least that courtesy.

Carrie Bishop drew herself up against a palm tree and caught her breath, though by all laws of biology she shouldn't be so winded. It wasn't the brisk walk that had started her blood pumping and her lungs heaving. No, it was the man she'd walked away from who had caused all these strange physiological reactions.

Her afternoon certainly had gotten off to an odd start. Accused of sabotage one minute and invited to a private diving lesson the next, and all by a man who gave new meaning to the phrase "tall, dark and handsome." His thick, dark hair was luxuriously wavy, even when wet, and Carrie had felt the insane urge to run her fingers through it when he sat next to her on the pier. And his mustache, which she had thought so dastardly-looking when she first laid eyes on him, now struck her as a particularly intriguing feature.

She had never seen eyes quite that green before, nor a specimen of the male human body quite that perfect, nor a swimsuit quite that brief! No wonder her heart rate was accelerated.

When Myra had told her how experienced and capable Jack Harrington was, Carrie had pictured someone a little more like Lloyd Bridges. The man couldn't be more than thirty-five.

Absently she tucked a tendril of blond hair into her thick ponytail and plotted what she would do next, now that she'd eliminated scuba diving. No matter; she had a whole island to explore.

Instead of heading down the heavily populated Quarter Moon Beach, she walked to the other side of the pier, where the beach was rough and untamed. There were no sunbathers here to step around, she mused, only large outcroppings of rocks.

A flash of red caught her eye just ahead, where the beach curved out of sight, but when she squinted to see what it was, it had disappeared. Curious, she continued walking until she rounded the curve. And there, crouching behind a large rock, was a tall, dark-skinned boy, perhaps twelve years old, wearing red shorts and no shirt. The shorts and his close-cropped hair were wet, and he shivered in the shade of the rock.

"Hello," Carrie said in her usual friendly manner. "Been swimming, have you?"

The boy only nodded.

"You should be drying out in the sun. Aren't you cold?"

He shook his head, his hands fiddling with a white, disk-shaped object Carrie couldn't identify. "I'm not cold," he said.

It was obvious from looking at the boy and hearing him speak that he was no tourist. Despite the fact that he continued to eye her with barely concealed suspicion, Carrie was fascinated with him, as she'd been with all the island people she'd met since her arrival on St. Thomas. She found herself wanting to make conversation just so she could hear him talk with that intriguing calypso accent.

She leaned her hips against the rock and gazed out at the ocean. "My name's Carrie. What's yours?"

"Carrie?" The boy's voice cracked as he repeated her name.

"Carrie Bishop."

"I'm called Jolly," he said after a long pause, seeming to warm to her slightly. "Hey, lady, what were you doing talking to Jack Harrington?"

"You were watching me?" she asked, turning to look at him.

He shrank into the shadow of the rock. "Just by accident."

Carrie noted that by altering his voice to a slightly higher pitch, Jolly could create the illusion that he was younger than he'd seemed a moment before.

"You seem like a nice lady," Jolly continued. "I'd be careful if I were you about hanging around folks like Jack Harrington."

"Oh?" Now Carrie's curiosity was more than piqued.

"The island isn't always as safe and friendly as it appears."

"Yes, I'll remember that." Her eyes again fell on the strange white disk Jolly fiddled with. It seemed to be made of rough-edged fiberglass, about three inches in diameter...

"...it was used to drill a three-inch hole in the hull of my boat..."

Jack's words came back to her, and suddenly she put it all together. But by the time she opened her mouth to voice her suspicions, Jolly had taken off running down the beach, his long legs eating up the sand. She tried to follow him, but after only a few paces she lost sight of him as he was swallowed by the crowd on the other side of the pier.

She should do something, she realized, but what? One glance toward the pier told her that Jack had already cast off and was limping away on the crippled *Carrie*, too far out for her to catch. She could go to the police, but what could she tell them that wouldn't sound wacky? And then there was the matter of Jolly's warning not to associate with "folks like Jack Harrington," although as the most likely suspect for the sabotage, Jolly was scarcely trustworthy himself.

Perhaps she'd best not get involved. The last thing she needed was to embroil herself in shady dealings. She would try to forget the whole thing and get on with her vacation. With that thought firmly in place, she threw her tote bag over her shoulder, then winced at the pain. She'd let herself get sunburned.

It sure didn't take much of this tropical sun to inflict a lot of damage, Carrie mused grimly. She set off in the direction of Quarter Moon Beach and the concrete staircase that led up to the hotel. She intended to visit the drugstore and purchase a stronger variety of sunscreen.

A few minutes later, clutching a small sack containing a bottle of sunscreen and a new roll of film, Carrie punched anxiously at the elevator button. There were so many things to do, so much to experience in the Virgin Islands! Her impatience made mundane things such as waiting for elevators all the more irksome.

She was determined not to let any opportunities get by her during her ten-day vacation on St. Thomas. She had come to tackle the new and unusual, to be daring and adventurous. She might not be able to make up for the ten years of her life she had wasted, but that didn't mean she couldn't try.

The first thing she did when she got to her room was to jump into a cold shower. When she emerged five minutes later, shivering, she reached for her sunburn remedy and applied the cool, soothing cream to her inflamed shoulders. As she massaged the cream into her warm skin, she examined the rest of her body in the full-length mirror for evidence of other sunburned areas. She was a little bit pink all over, she had to admit, but it was nothing the cream couldn't fix.

Everything else Carrie's mirror told her was good. Her aerobics classes had paid off in new contours, especially striking in her revealing turquoise swimsuit. She could see muscle definition in her legs where before there had been only bland softness, and she would be willing to bet that if she tried on her ten-year-old wedding dress, it would be baggy.

Carrie wrinkled her nose at the thought of that frumpy wedding dress, the one her mother had insisted on, the one Web had praised so highly. It was stiff-necked and immobile, old-fashioned—and it epitomized her entire married life with Web Ashland. She vowed that when she returned home she would donate it to the nearest Goodwill store.

After giving herself one last appraising overview, she put on a red cotton dress that would protect her shoulders from the sun for the rest of the day. She consulted her guidebook for a place to grab a late lunch and decided upon the Mermaid, which advertised exotic seafood and appeared to be within walking distance of the hotel. Squid—yes, she'd never had squid. Since she'd been cheated out of her scuba class, she would eat squid this afternoon, instead.

Carrie stirred from a ridiculously vivid dream that featured a dashing pirate—not an unpleasant dream, surprisingly. She buried her head under the pillow, trying to recapture the images, but they seemed to slip just out of her reach.

A soft but persistent knock on the door intruded into her consciousness until she was fully awake—and fully aware of her uncomfortably sunburned skin.

"I'm coming. Just a minute." She sat upright, wincing at the pain even that slight movement brought to her tight skin. She scanned the room for her kimono, which she finally found flung over a chair. Gingerly she slipped her arms into the soft purple garment and belted it loosely at her waist as she made her way to the door.

Forgetting to be cautious, she opened the door without looking through the peephole.

And there stood Jack Harrington, a pirate conjured out of her dreams. A pirate wearing jams, a Hawaiian shirt and flip-flops.

His face broke into a sheepish grin. "Hi. Did I wake you?"

"No, I—" The skeptical look he gave her cut her off. "All right, yes, I was asleep. I never realized how strenuous a vacation could be."

"And you've only been here one day," Jack added. "Can I come in? I need to talk to you about something."

Mustering a sleepy smile, Carrie opened the door wider to admit him, realizing belatedly that the room was a wreck. The booty from her recent shopping spree in Charlotte Amalie lay scattered all around the floor and the bed, along with various items of clothing she'd tried on and discarded. Oddly, she wasn't the least bit frightened to be alone in a hotel room with this virtual stranger. She supposed she should have been, given Jolly's warning, but Carrie wasn't prone to suspicion without good reason. And Jack did work for the hotel, after all.

Jack surveyed the room, amusement evident on his face. His gaze rested on each item for a moment: a plastic model of a pirate's ship, several bright silk scarves, a bottle of Caribbean rum, a huge pink conch shell and several smaller ones, a leather coin purse, a candle in the shape of a palm tree, several T-shirts, souvenir coffee cups and a night-light made from a sea urchin. "You *have* only been here one day, right?" he asked. "You'll empty the shops by midweek if you keep this up."

Carrie laughed self-consciously, picking up several empty paper sacks and wadding them into the wastebasket. "I have a lot of nieces and nephews who'll be expecting presents when I get back." Inwardly she cringed, knowing she sounded like a typical tourist, but that was what she was, so she might as well not pretend otherwise.

Jack's gaze fell on Carrie herself and rested there an uncomfortably long time. "What are you doing for that sunburn?" he finally asked.

"I've got some cream for it." She wished he would stop looking at her that way. It wasn't the sort of look she would call an ogle or a leer, but whatever he was doing, it made her acutely aware of her rumpled and sleep-worn appearance. One hand automatically went up to run fingers through her tousled hair and the other went to the neckline of her robe, which now felt much too revealing.

"I know what will help. Do you mind?" He sat on the edge of the bed and picked up the telephone receiver.

"If you can help my sunburn, then by all means . . ." She nodded toward the phone and shrugged. She doubted anything more could be done to alleviate her pain. She wondered again why he had come to see her—surely not to talk about her afflictions.

Jack spoke into the phone briefly as Carrie continued to tidy the room. She recalled her meeting with the boy Jolly, knowing that she would have to tell Jack about it despite her wish to keep out of this sabotage business.

When he finished his phone conversation, she launched immediately into the story, describing as many details as possible but tactfully leaving out the aspersions Jolly had cast at Jack.

Jack listened with rapt attention as she wove her tale about the funny character she'd met on the beach.

"Jolly, huh? No last name?"

"No. I'm sorry I wasn't a more skillful detective, but it took me a while to realize that the thing he was holding—"

Jack held up his hand. "It's all right. You've given me someplace to start. Jolly is an unusual name, so perhaps I can track him down."

Silence hung between them for a moment until it occurred to Carrie to ask, "Mr. Harrington, I'm still puzzled. Why did you come here?"

"Call me Jack. And I'm here because I wanted to ask you if...well, if you'd have dinner with me."

"Why?" Carrie could have kicked herself. Why hadn't she managed to say something more appropriate?

"Why?" Jack repeated. "Because...because I thought it might be fun. Do I have to have a reason to want to take a pretty woman out to dinner?"

"I...I don't know," she hedged as she struggled to control her illogically racing heart. "With this sunburn and all—"

"I'm going to fix the sunburn."

"But Myra signed me up for the rumba contest this evening in the Blue Moon Lounge..." *Here I go again,* she thought in despair, *tourist city.*

"You know how to rumba?"

"No, but I'm willing to learn. After all, I probably couldn't rumba in Des Moines."

"What if I promise to teach you how to rumba? Will you have dinner with me?"

She gazed at him another heart-stopping moment, unable to comprehend why he was being so persistent. She'd run out of excuses, although she wasn't sure she needed any more. The idea of having dinner with Jack was infinitely more appealing than sitting alone in the hotel dining room. Jolly's warning be damned.

"All right. Fix the sunburn and throw in rumba lessons, and I'll have dinner with you."

"Excellent." He rose to answer the door almost before the knock sounded. A room-service waiter stood holding a glass bottle. Jack pulled a bill from his pocket and tipped the man, then turned to Carrie and handed her the bottle.

She read the label: vinegar. She lifted one eyebrow skeptically. "Do I drink it or bathe in it?"

"Wash the lotion off your skin, then splash the vinegar on the way you would, uh, after-shave."

Carrie wrinkled her nose. "I'm not in the habit of using after-shave. Are you sure about this?"

"Positive. I'll see you at eight."

Carrie gazed at the door for at least a minute after Jack had disappeared through it. *You ninny!* she berated herself. *A good-looking guy comes into your room, throws you a few compliments, and suddenly your brains are addled.*

What was she thinking, accepting a date with a stranger in an unfamiliar place? She hadn't come to the Virgin Islands to meet a man. If anything, she had embarked on this vacation to prove beyond a doubt that she could enjoy life to its fullest *without* a man.

Web had been the center of her existence during the ten years they were together. She was only nineteen when they were married, and he was nearly twenty years her senior, a handsome, successful orthopedic surgeon. He'd courted her relentlessly from the first time he'd seen her on campus at the University of Iowa, where he was a guest lecturer.

Carrie had been swept off her feet by the debonair, sophisticated doctor. Still, his marriage proposal had been unexpected, and Carrie had hesitated, wondering if she shouldn't finish school first. Then her parents got wind of Web's proposal, and they were so enthusiastic about the marriage that the decision was more or less taken out of her hands. Wedding plans were made, Carrie was swept along in the excitement, and before long she was Mrs. Web Ashland.

It hadn't been a *bad* marriage, Carrie reflected, just an incredibly dull one. The whirlwind courtship ended with a thud when the honeymoon was over, leaving Carrie confused and hurt.

For ten years, Carrie tried to put some spark into their relationship. She did her level best to make Web happy, but as the years passed, it became increasingly apparent that she and Web were ill matched. Still, she would never have left him, for she was a firm believer in the sanctity of marriage vows. And Web was kind in an offhand way, if not a particularly exciting mate. She had settled into the marriage, resigned herself to it and devoted most of her energy to trying to improve it.

Web's sudden departure a year ago had shocked and devastated Carrie. For a time she believed the fault was hers. She hadn't tried hard enough, she had told herself. Even Carrie's parents had hinted that she had done something to drive Web away.

But her outlook had changed over the past year. She had turned down Web's generous settlement offer, opting instead to make it on her own. Away from the sheltering influence of a husband who had, if nothing else, provided for her, she'd finally come to realize that being the director of her own life was infinitely more satisfying than dependency on a disinterested husband, no matter how wealthy and successful he was.

Now that she'd learned to create her own happiness, she was beginning to feel whole and complete as she never had before. The last thing she needed was to get involved with another man.

Get involved? Who was she kidding? She'd be gone in ten days, back to her uneventful life in Des Moines, and Jack Harrington would still be here, racing around in his boat and wrestling sharks—or whatever it was he did. Surely there was nothing wrong with having dinner with him. No one could blame Carrie for wanting to build some exciting memories while she was here. And Jack epitomized excitement in her mind.

She undressed and gently washed away the lotion as Jack had directed. And then, much to her distaste, she applied the sour-smelling vinegar to every sunburned inch of herself. Surprisingly, it cooled her skin immediately and left an invigorating tingle in place of the irritating heat.

"All right, Jack Harrington," she said aloud. "So you were right. I hope you don't mind rumbaing with a woman whose perfume is Eau De Salad Dressing."

Jack couldn't help whistling tunelessly as he waited for the elevator to take him to the lobby. He still didn't know what had possessed him to ask Carrie Bishop to dinner, but he didn't regret it. How long had it been since he'd allowed himself an evening of leisure with a beautiful woman? Or maybe he should be asking himself how long it had been since he'd looked at a woman and thought her beautiful?

He had begun to think he'd lost the ability to see beauty. For the past six years he had approached his work, and life in general, with a single-minded determination that kept him from appreciating the aesthetic aspects of living. But gazing at Carrie, he had felt the faint strumming of a chord inside him left silent too long.

Though he knew little about Carrie Bishop, she seemed the antithesis of the dark thoughts that haunted him. Blond and fair, sweet-tempered, she exhibited a whimsical sense of wonder about the world. He used to have that sense of wonder, too. What had happened to it?

As the elevator doors whisked open and he stepped inside, he found himself looking forward to an enjoyable evening. The sensation was novel.

Downstairs he found Myra absorbed in the task of filing brochures in her desk, which sat in a corner of the plush lobby. She flipped through the files with graceful, almond-skinned hands, dropping each brochure efficiently into its appropriate manila folder. Only when Jack cleared his throat did she look up, then she smiled almost as if she knew a secret.

"So, it's you again," she said, pushing the pile of slick brochures aside and taking her chair. She surveyed Jack with jet-black eyes. "Was Ms. Bishop able to help you?"

"Help me?" he repeated. Then he realized she was referring to his boat. "Yes, as a matter of fact. Say, Myra, have you ever heard of a kid by the name of Jolly hanging around here on the beach? A local boy, about twelve years old?"

Myra's delicate eyebrows drew together in thought for a moment. "No, I don't believe so. Why?"

"That's who sabotaged my boat."

"A kid?"

Jack shrugged. "Not to change the subject, but where would you take someone to dinner for an evening to remember?"

Myra turned up just one corner of her red-glossed lips. "It wouldn't matter. No one forgets an evening with me."

Then her eyes narrowed. "Are you having dinner with Carrie Bishop?"

Jack neither confirmed nor denied, but apparently Myra didn't need him to.

"I had a bad feeling when you came to me looking for her with all that mumbo jumbo about her being a witness to a crime. Jack, you know perfectly well the hotel's policy on employees socializing with the guests. In eight months you've never once hit on a guest. Why start now?"

Jack drummed his fingers on the desk, wondering what he'd done to set Myra off. He paused before replying, carefully screening the irritation out of his voice. "In the first place, I'm not a hotel employee, I'm contract labor. In the second place I'm not 'hitting on' Carrie Bishop. Apparently she's not an experienced traveler, and she doesn't need to be wasting her time at hotel rumba contests with senior citizens." He paused again, staring at Myra pointedly. "I merely want to show her a place that isn't in all the guide books."

Myra folded her arms and eyed Jack skeptically.

"I'm not planning to seduce her, so you can stop looking at me that way. Don't you think I know an innocent when I see one?"

"Innocent, huh? What would you say if I told you that before her divorce she was married for ten years?"

Now it was Jack's turn to look skeptical. "Ten years? Come on, she can't be a day over twenty-five. Anyway, how would you know?"

"She's thirty. And I know because I spent more than an hour with her this morning, signing her up for all kinds of excursions and activities. I'm telling you, she is a tour director's dream. But you're right about one thing—she's never traveled before. Her husband was some big-shot surgeon who earned a ton of money but apparently never spent a penny of it to make her happy.''

Jack clicked his tongue against the roof of his mouth and shook his head. ''Myra, I'm surprised at you. It's not like you to gossip, especially about the guests.''

''Well, I thought you should know what you're getting yourself into. And if she were here I'd tell her a thing or two about you. Listen, Jack, I've seen diving instructors come and I've seen them go. They usually leave after some unpleasant incident with a female guest. Now you and this Carrie Bishop are going to make some sparks fly if you don't stay away from each other. I felt the chemistry at work the moment she mentioned your name this afternoon—''

''She mentioned my name?''

''She was kind enough to inform me that your boat was out of commission and your scuba classes canceled, which is more than you did.''

''Myra . . . Myra, I won't cause any trouble for her, I promise. One dinner. I'll have her home before midnight. Now will you drop the inquisition and give me a useful suggestion for dinner?''

Myra treated him to a challenging stare for a moment longer before she relented. ''Okay, you win. I'll drop it for now. Why don't you take her to Billy Bones? That's no tourist trap, and it's always been one of my favorites.''

Impulsively Jack took both Myra's hands and kissed them. ''Billy Bones, of course! Thanks, sweetheart. Oh, and Myra?''

''Hmm?''

''Do you know how to rumba?''

''Of course. Doesn't everybody?''

''Can you teach me how before this evening?''

She let out a long-suffering sigh. ''Even if I was inclined to, I couldn't. I have a hot date tonight with a very wealthy

European. Claude came sailing into the harbor yesterday on the finest-looking yacht you ever did see."

Jack shook his head and smiled. "How do you do it? How do you always manage to hook up with the rich ones the moment they make port?"

"I don't have to lift a finger, sugar. They just find me."

Chapter Two

This time Carrie was prepared when Jack knocked on her door. Her clothes were neatly hung in the closet; the bed was made; she had consolidated all her souvenirs into one large shopping bag and had shoved it under the bed, along with her empty suitcases.

After a great deal of deliberation, she had finally decided to wear a sleeveless sheath dress made of a kitten-soft white cotton knit. Though the skirt was slender, it had a modest slit that would allow her at least some freedom of movement for dancing.

A year ago, when she was still married, she would have thought it was a dress *other* women wore, women who went dining and dancing and to cocktail parties and theater presentations and to the symphony—but not a dress for plain, domestic Mrs. Ashland. What an idiot she'd been! In her effort to be the perfect, docile wife she'd never made a single demand of her conservative, antisocial husband, not even a mild one. In the process she had not only consigned herself to a dreadfully dull life, she had bored Web to distraction until he had no other choice but to jump ship.

What would he think if he could see her now, attired so fashionably in a dress that actually made her look—dare she even think it—sexy? Well, maybe not sexy, exactly, but it did cling to her curves in a pleasing way.

She swept her wavy hair up into a loose chignon and secured it with several pins. The crowning touch was an antique gold comb studded with paste sapphires. Looking at it, she thought of Web again. He'd dutifully bought her various trinkets over the years for birthdays and anniversaries, but the comb was the only gift that sparkled with originality, as if he'd picked it out with her specifically in mind. Carrie wore it often—not out of sentimentality, but because it suited her, fake gems and all.

Jack was seven minutes late, just late enough to start her wondering whether she'd dreamed the whole episode this afternoon. No, there was the bottle of vinegar on the dresser to prove he'd been here. Then the knock sounded, and her heart nearly leaped out of her throat.

Maybe this isn't such a good idea, she thought, irritated that she didn't have better control over her physical reactions. But when she pulled the door open, any regrets she might have had about accepting Jack's invitation vanished.

"Good evening," he said with a touch of formality that reminded Carrie of one of those romantic movies from the 1940s. "If I'd known how lovely you'd look I'd have gotten here sooner."

They stood in the doorway for several seconds, silently appraising one another. Carrie took in the wavy black hair, the crisp khaki slacks so well suited to his leanness, the unconventionally tailored blue shirt, which did such nice things to his broad shoulders. Finally Jack ended the standoff by magically producing a flower from behind his back, a single pink hibiscus blossom.

Taking the flower with murmured thanks, Carrie pulled the door wider to give Jack entrance. She allowed herself another moment to absorb the pleasure of having an attractive man pay her a compliment, something that hadn't happened in many years. Then it dawned on her that the flower looked suspiciously like those that covered the huge potted bushes downstairs in the lobby, and she had to smile.

"What? What is it?" Jack asked immediately.

"Nothing," she fibbed as she pinned the delicate flower to the shoulder of her sleeveless dress. "I'm just feeling a little giddy tonight. Vacation rush, if you will. There, that doesn't look silly, does it?" She turned to show him her handiwork with the flower.

Jack shook his head, his expression serious. "Nothing about you looks silly."

Carrie laughed nervously. "I saw Myra a little while ago on my way to the drugstore to buy...an essential." Panty hose, but she wasn't going to tell him *that*. "She happened to mention the real reason you came looking for me this afternoon."

"And I suppose she also told you I was a no-good pirate?"

Pirate. Funny he should choose that word after her dream. "No, she said nothing of the kind."

"So now you know, the dinner invitation was made on impulse. I don't regret it." He stood decisively. "Are you ready?"

She nodded. Her small satin evening bag sat on the dresser, containing the room key, some lip gloss, a comb, her passport and her traveler's checks—she believed in being prepared. She picked up the bag along with a delicate, pearl-buttoned cardigan that matched her dress. Then Jack took her arm, and they headed for the door like Cinderella and her prince on the way to a ball. But just as Carrie switched off the light, Jack paused, his hand frozen on the doorknob.

"What's that scent?"

"It's vinegar, and I don't want to hear a word—"

"No, not vinegar." He came closer to her in the darkness, until she could feel his breath against her neck, then on her hair. "It's apples. Your hair smells like green apples. I'm right, aren't I?"

"I . . . I guess so. It's just a shampoo I pick up at the grocery . . . store . . ." Her thoughts became muddled as his lips barely touched her neck then made a feather-light trail to her collarbone. No words would form in her throat, so she communicated her mixed reaction by squeezing Jack's arm until her knuckles ached from the pressure. What was he trying to do to her?

As suddenly as the moment came, it lifted. Jack opened the door and gently guided her through it with a hand at her waist, then closed it again. The *snick* of the lock sounded strangely loud to Carrie in the quiet hallway. Then Jack was talking again, as if nothing earth-shattering had passed between them.

"I hope you like seafood. The place we're going has the freshest, the absolute best on the whole island. The owner used to be the chef on board some Greek oil tycoon's yacht."

Carrie attempted to shake off the spell Jack had cast over her. "I love seafood," she finally managed in a somewhat normal voice, "especially what I've tasted here so far. Des Moines doesn't get . . . Oh, never mind, I don't want to talk about Des Moines."

"Des Moines isn't such a bad place," Jack said. "I went through there once on my way to Lake Michigan, and it struck me as an attractive little town."

"Boring little town," Carrie corrected.

"Then why do you live there?"

She pondered this as they made their way through the luxurious lobby and out the glass doors into the warm, exotically scented evening. She'd never seriously considered living elsewhere, though she wasn't sure why. Finally she shrugged. "I didn't have much choice about where to live, really. I grew up in Iowa, went to school there, and now my work is there, not to mention my family. . . ." She'd left out the part about living ten years with a man who was firmly entrenched in Des Moines.

They paused beside a low wall that flanked one side of the hotel's ostentatious front entrance. "Wait here," Jack instructed. "I'll go get our transportation and pick you up."

"I can walk to the parking lot with you," Carrie objected.

"No, I want you to save your feet for dancing," he said firmly, playfully pushing down on her shoulders until she had no choice but to sit on the wall. "Be right back." He took off at a sprint through the parking lot.

About two minutes later he reappeared, riding a bright red motor scooter. He pulled up in front of Carrie with a flourish and jumped off. "What do you think of her?"

"I think," said Carrie, who had sprung to her feet in surprise the moment she'd seen the scooter, "that I can't ride on *that* thing in *this* dress."

"Sure you can. Can't you just sorta . . . hike up the skirt a little?"

"It's too narrow. I'd be arrested for indecent ex—po—sure—" She dissolved into hopeless laughter. "Oh, Jack, I guess I should have been prepared for something like this.

You could have warned me, you know, and then I could have worn a different dress.''

He looked at her pointedly. ''Then I'm glad I didn't warn you.''

Carrie felt herself blush at the sudden heat in Jack's clear green eyes. She busied herself with donning her sweater, careful not to crush the hibiscus bloom. ''I suppose I could ride sidesaddle,'' she suggested, returning to the problem at hand.

''Sure you can.'' He smiled confidently as he handed her a small crash helmet, which she put on. The helmet made her sapphire comb dig into her scalp, but she didn't really care. She viewed this incident as another adventure, another chance to experience something new. Certainly she'd never ridden a scooter.

''I'm not complaining, mind you, but don't you have a car?'' she asked as Jack positioned her on the back of the black leather seat, with her feet perched on the running board.

''Not anymore.'' He climbed on board in front of her. ''I sold it to help pay for my boat. Hold on tight, now.''

She put her fingers gingerly through his belt loops and sent up a silent prayer.

''I said *tight*.'' He reached behind him, grabbed each of her wrists and pulled her arms around his rib cage. ''There. You'll thank me later.'' With that he put the scooter in gear and they zipped out of the parking lot.

The sky was turning to peach and auburn with the impending dusk. It was so breathtakingly beautiful that Carrie sighed aloud, thinking she must be the luckiest, most carefree person on earth at that moment. Lucky, that is, until a sudden lurch of the scooter nearly unseated her.

''Watch the sharp turns,'' Carrie yelled as they careened around yet another bend in the road, but she feared her words were lost in the wind. She tightened her grip and sent up a more fervent prayer than the last.

If she hadn't been so scared, she might have more thoroughly enjoyed the feel of her breasts pressed against Jack's strong back, the rough texture of his shirt against her cheek and the tangy scent of his after-shave. But all those pleasant sensations were noted and filed away for later consideration. Carrie spent most of her conscious thought fearing for her life.

They slowed at the top of a hill, surrounded by dense tropical foliage and not much else. The scooter putted along, and Jack peered through the growing darkness into the trees by the side of the road, apparently looking for something. He cut the engine.

"Why are we stopping here?" Carrie asked, wondering what other little surprises Jack might have up his sleeve.

He helped her off the scooter and took her helmet. Then he proceeded to walk the scooter off the road and behind a stand of banana trees, where he locked it up with a heavy chain.

"We have to walk from here," he explained matter-of-factly, taking Carrie's arm and guiding her through a gap in the trees.

Was he crazy? she wondered. Why would he take her for a hike through the jungle when she was dressed so inappropriately? Then she saw an ancient-looking stone staircase leading down the hill, and she felt a small measure of relief.

"This restaurant we're going to—it doesn't have a road leading to it?" she ventured.

"It does, but ... oops, here we go, single file." The staircase had narrowed, and Carrie forged on ahead, Jack's warm hands applying the slightest pressure to her shoulders from behind. "The road we were on would eventually have gotten us there," Jack continued explaining, "but to follow it would have been the extreme long way around. It meanders all over the island before ending up at our destination, which is only a few yards away."

A few yards. What a strange place this island was. Carrie was used to streets being laid out in neat blocks. If you wanted to get somewhere, you went *x* number of blocks one way and *y* the other, and you were there. The island method of arriving at a destination bordered on the bizarre, but she couldn't deny it was kind of fun.

A few more steps, and they emerged from the foliage to find themselves on an empty beach. Carrie stopped and stared out over the ocean at a sky streaked with violet and vermilion from the last rays of sunlight. She was suddenly amazed once again that she was actually on a tropical island in the Caribbean. Back home it was probably snowing.

Jack sat on the bottom step of the staircase and proceeded to remove his shoes and socks.

"What *are* you doing?" Carrie asked.

"Walking on the beach is much easier without shoes."

Carrie shrugged and followed suit, slipping her stockinged feet out of the white pumps. Nothing could surprise her at this point. They walked side by side down the beach, carrying their shoes. The wet sand felt deliciously cool on the bottoms of Carrie's feet, even though her hose were getting soaked.

It seemed perfectly natural for Jack to take her hand, so she accepted the gesture without comment. Her own hand felt warm and secure in his larger one.

"Are you having fun?" Jack asked suddenly. "I know this isn't your typical dinner date, but I thought you might enjoy something a little different—"

"This is different, all right," she replied, suppressing her laughter.

"You don't like it?"

He sounded so disappointed that Carrie didn't have the heart to withhold her approval any longer.

"I love it," she answered with all sincerity. "But how much further? Is that our destination?" She pointed to a glimmering of lights ahead of them.

"That's it, a mere five minutes away—three if we run."

"Run?" Carrie imagined herself hiking up her clingy skirt and sprinting down the beach. But then she saw Jack's teasing smile.

"No, I'd rather walk," he said softly.

Billy Bones, as the restaurant was called, was larger and more crowded than Carrie had expected, given its hard-to-reach location. Perched on the beach in a protected cove, it was a square building that appeared to be made out of bamboo. Attached to the building was a roomy, partially covered desk, where a steel band was just setting up.

Beyond the deck was a private pier, lined with large sailboats and cruisers of every size and description, alongside tiny motorboats and one dinghy. Anchored farther out were two grand-looking yachts.

"Do most people arrive here by boat?" Carrie asked, eyeing every inch of the place with curiosity as she and Jack crossed the last few feet of sand to the entrance. She slipped into her shoes before mounting the two steps to the door.

"A boat is the easiest way to get here," he answered, quickly donning his socks and shoes. "We would have come here in mine if she weren't out of commission."

Jack opened the door, and Carrie entered an exotic, tropical world, complete with caged parrots and lush greenery. The place captured her imagination—and her appetite. An incredibly mouth-watering aroma greeted her, wafting through the restaurant from the huge grill that dominated the dining room. A casually dressed maître d' greeted Jack by name and showed them to a cozy table with an excellent view of the fascinating grill.

"I'm sure I didn't see anything about this place in my guidebook," Carrie said as Jack seated her.

"The owner doesn't cater to the tourist trade," Jack explained.

"Terrific. I wonder what he would think of me."

"You're not a tourist. You're a . . . a guest of the island."

Carrie smiled, genuinely touched. "That's a very lovely sentiment. Now, what's good to eat?" She opened her menu, but found she couldn't concentrate on it. Several tendrils of her hair had escaped their pins and were tickling her forehead and cheeks. She felt a compelling need to at least look in a mirror and check the damage inflicted by the wind and the crash helmet. She excused herself and went in search of a ladies' room.

The plain but serviceable bathroom mirror revealed what Carrie had feared: her hair was a wreck. Quickly she dismantled the chignon, combed her hair and put it all back together again until it was as sleek and tidy as it had been when she started out.

She renewed her pale pink lip gloss and finally, satisfied with her appearance, she gave her hair one final pat before exiting the room—and running smack into a man's chest. The collision dislodged her bag from her hand. It dropped to the floor, spilling its entire contents.

"Oh, do be careful," the man said in a heavy French accent, his steadying hands on her shoulders.

"I believe the men's is at the other end of the hall," Carrie said helpfully, stooping to retrieve her belongings, but the man put a restraining hand on her shoulder and began scooping up her things himself.

"I'll get this, it was my fault. But I wasn't looking for the lavatory." He put her purse into her hands. "I came here because I wanted to talk to you privately, Miss Bishop."

She had started to turn away from him, but now she whirled and faced him squarely. She was alarmed by his use of her name but curious to know what he wanted.

"Is there something I can do for you, Mr...."

He ignored her obvious request for a name. "You can tell me what your business is with Jack Harrington." The voice was soft but held a note of insistence that bothered Carrie, as if he believed she owed him something.

It was too dark in the hallway for her to get a clear look at his face. She had an impression of height and bulkiness that was well disguised by expertly tailored clothes. His after-shave smelled heavy and expensive, and some sort of round, gold object dangled at his throat, glinting even in the meager light. She saw a wide, gold band at his wrist, too, and a diamond pinky ring. This ostentatious showing fostered an instant dislike for the man in Carrie's mind. That, and a lack of good manners.

"Why should I tell you anything?" she replied after a long pause. "I don't know you from Adam." She resisted the urge to simply flee. Her self-preservation instinct was strong, but her curiosity was stronger. First the boy Jolly had warned her about Jack, and now this Frenchman was trying to interrogate her on the same subject. Even Myra had tried to question her about her choice of dinner companion, though Carrie had deftly avoided the tour director's most probing inquiries.

"Jack is wanted by the authorities," the man said quietly. "And I am a duly appointed government official heading up an investigation. You can either answer my question now or you'll be brought in to headquarters for questioning later, a most boring and time-consuming procedure. Now I repeat, what is your business with Mr. Harrington?''

Carrie felt the blood drain from her face. Good sense dictated that she cooperate with this man, who appeared to have the force of the law behind him. Brushes with the authorities were not her style; she'd never been charged with so much as a parking violation. But something about the Frenchman didn't quite ring true, though she couldn't have said exactly what it was.

Without warning, taunting words sprang from Carrie's lips in a tone of voice that didn't sound like her at all. "If Jack is wanted, why don't you arrest him? He's right out there." She pointed toward the dining room.

"This is a complicated case, Miss Bishop, which requires delicate handling. It wouldn't serve my purposes to arrest him now."

"How do you know my name?" she demanded.

"I...saw it on your passport when I put your things back in your handbag. I've answered your questions. Are you going to answer mine?"

Carrie thought about it for one moment longer. "No. No, I'm not. Good evening." With that she turned and walked away from the Frenchman as fast as she could with dignity, her heart pounding so loudly she was sure everyone in the restaurant could hear it. She must be crazy, casting a suspicious light on herself and possibly placing herself in jeopardy by deliberately sidestepping the question.

But what right did this man have to question her like some criminal, when she'd done nothing wrong? If he'd been more forthright with her, if he'd told her who he was and what *kind* of government official he was, and exactly what Jack was wanted for, she might have been more cooperative. He hadn't even offered to show her any identification! Instead of making an honest request, the man had tried to intimidate her because he thought she was weak and naive. Carrie fumed silently. All the more reason not to like him.

Anyway, as crazy as it seemed, she did like Jack. Her instincts told her that whatever he was involved in—and obviously he was involved in something—he was no criminal. She wasn't sure how she knew that, but she knew it as surely as she knew her own name.

Jack drummed his fingers on the table and resisted the urge to cut a slice of the warm, fragrant French bread the waiter had just placed in front of him. His stomach was grumbling, but he would wait for Carrie.

How long could one trip to the ladies' room take? He hadn't pegged Carrie as the type who spent hours in front of the mirror—she didn't need to, for one thing. In her case, nature couldn't be much improved upon. He rather liked the way her hair had looked after their scooter ride, a disarrayed mass of gold framing her face. The style, or lack thereof, made her look wild and full of abandon. He suspected she was neither, so he wasn't surprised when she finally reappeared, every strand of hair neatly in place.

"Sorry I took so long," she apologized, removing the sweater and draping it over the back of her chair before taking her seat and perusing the menu.

Jack knew the menu by heart, so he spent the next couple of minutes idly buttering a piece of the long-awaited bread while studying Carrie's bared shoulders and arms, the hollow of her throat and the faintest hint of the valley that disappeared into the neckline of her dress. In the soft torchlight of the restaurant, her sunburn appeared burnished to a rich tan. The longer he looked at her, the more tantalizing she became.

"Mmm, everything sounds great," she said, looking up at him after a minute or two. "Which would you recommend, fresh shark, stir-fry marlin or broiled yellowtail?"

Jack stirred himself from his appreciative contemplation long enough to answer coherently. "Yellowtail is my personal favorite, especially the way it's prepared here. It literally melts in your mouth."

Carrie took his recommendation, and they dispatched the waiter to bring them both yellowtail fillets, accompanied by a green salad and fried plantains.

Once the waiter was out of earshot, Carrie put her chin in her hands and gazed directly at Jack with curious gray-blue eyes, one corner of her pink-glossed lips turned up as if she were debating whether to speak.

Jack stared back, unaccountably pleased at her frank appraisal of him. He remained deliberately silent, giving her every opportunity to speak her mind. Finally she did.

"I know it's really no concern of mine, Jack, but are you by any chance involved in some sort of...illicit activities?"

He hadn't known what to expect, but it certainly wasn't a question like that. He responded quite naturally with a hearty laugh and an unqualified no.

"But you must be involved in something, or else why would anyone want to sabotage your boat?" Carrie had leaned forward slightly, and her enchantingly guileless eyes widened with curiosity.

"What if I told you I was into drug smuggling and gunrunning?" he ventured. He was testing her, to see exactly how adventure-starved she was.

But she merely smiled and shook her head. "I wouldn't believe you. You're absolutely not the type."

"Oh? And how would you know? How many drug smugglers and gunrunners have you known personally?"

"Counting you? None. Come on now, I didn't mean something *that* illicit. But is there . . . a warrant out for your arrest, something like that?"

Honestly, he couldn't tell whether she was serious or not. He decided to answer her more directly this time. "Carrie, I assure you I'm not wanted by anyone. I run a little diving business in the Virgin Islands and I keep to myself. I'm as baffled by this sabotage stuff as anyone."

She leaned back in her chair, her arms crossed, looking like the cat that got the cream. "If that's true, then why did you assume this afternoon that I was interested in your sonar equipment? Or where you keep your maps?"

She had him there. He remembered now that during his fit of outrage that afternoon he carelessly *had* mentioned sonar and maps. Carrie hadn't missed a trick.

"The sonar is used to help me locate certain physical features on the ocean floor. Once I find them, I map them. It's sort of a hobby with me. See, a very simple explanation."

"What sort of physical features?"

She wasn't going to let him off the hook. What would she think if he told her he went diving for sunken treasure? He'd just as soon not admit it. Most people reacted rather strangely to his chosen profession. They either contracted an immediate case of hysterical gold fever and offered to become his partner or they thought he was a crackpot. He didn't want to know which category Carrie would fall into.

He needed a distraction—and suddenly he had one. He pushed his chair back and stood. "The band is starting up. I think we have time for one dance before our dinner arrives. Shall we?"

She smiled sweetly at him. "Sure." They walked hand in hand to the outdoor deck. The steel band struck up a slow rendition of "Jamaica Farewell," and all at once Carrie was in his arms for an easy two-step. Jack didn't consider himself the world's most gifted dancer, but Carrie seemed to float with him, and his own steps became almost effortless.

"You dance well," he said, stating a simple truth.

"Mrs. Elvira Lipscomb's School of Ballroom Dance, seventh grade. I seldom get the chance to demonstrate my appreciable abilities. Waltz, fox-trot, two-step, polka—but no rumba. And definitely no tango. I suppose Mrs. Lipscomb didn't consider those types of dances refined enough for young ladies."

He pulled her closer and inhaled deeply of the intriguing green-apple scent of her hair. "I'll teach you to tango," he murmured, though it was an idle promise. He didn't know how to tango any better than he could rumba.

The next song was slower paced, and Jack welcomed the opportunity to put both arms around Carrie and fit her to him as they swayed gently back and forth. He could feel her every curve against him through the thin material of her dress, and suddenly he was achingly aroused.

She was warm from her sunburn, but he had the distinct impression that she was radiating an extra measure of heat that was entirely her own. He could feel it right through his clothes.

Her hands rested lightly on his shoulder blades, like twin birds that would take flight if they were even mildly startled. His hands glided up and down her back, barely touching so as not to aggravate her sunburn. Still, he closed his eyes and tried to memorize every plane and angle of her through the soft knit she wore. His hands itched to slide under the dress and touch bare flesh, to curve around those soft, inviting breasts. The fact that he couldn't only increased his unexpectedly sharp craving for her.

She nestled closer to him, until he could feel her breath against his neck. "Jack?" It was a mere whisper.

"Yes?"

"What sort of physical features on the ocean floor do you map?"

Damn. He thought he'd outmaneuvered her, but it appeared Carrie was more persistent than he was clever.

"I map shipwrecks," he said as the song ended. He let his arm linger around her slender waist as they made their way back to the table. And because that admission was bound to generate more questions from the inquisitive Carrie, he decided to elaborate. "I'm a marine archaeologist. I study the history of shipping and maritime laws and trade routes and piracy, and particularly shipwrecks. Currently I'm researching wrecks in the Virgin Islands for the university here, and I run the diving classes to supplement the rather sketchy grant funds I receive. Absolutely nothing illicit or illegal in that."

Carrie seemed impressed with his lengthy admission, and for a few moments all she could do was stare at him with raised eyebrows. He pulled out her chair for her, satisfied that his discourse had finally silenced her questions.

Their food came, and they spent the next few minutes sampling, nodding and sighing in delight, their discussion of Jack's underwater work apparently dismissed. Billy Bones's yellowtail was flawless, as usual.

"Are these things supposed to taste like potatoes?" Carrie asked, poking at her plantains with a fork.

"They're more like bananas," Jack explained. "But they're as common as potatoes around here. Sometimes they're served as dessert, with ice cream. I've seen them..." He stopped when he realized Carrie was looking at him again with that quizzical expression, as if something was on her mind besides her vegetables.

"I'll tell you more about myself, if you really want to know," he said. "I didn't mean to be so mysterious before. It's just that some people find my chosen field kind of strange, so I'm not in the habit of sharing it. You don't really believe I'm some sort of pirate, do you?"

She sighed. "No, I don't. But I do have one more question for you, and I'd appreciate a straight answer."

"Anything. Shoot."

"Is there a Frenchman looking for you?"

Jack paused before answering, giving the question serious consideration. "I don't think so," he replied in all honesty. "I don't recall any recent dealings with anyone French. Why? *I'd* appreciate a straight answer, too."

"I bumped into this French guy on my way back from the rest room. He said he was a government official, that you were a wanted man, and that I'd best tell him what my business was with you."

Jack's first response was outrage that someone with a grudge against him would go after a completely innocent third party like Carrie. "Good Lord, did he actually threaten you? Why didn't you tell me right away?" Then he thought about it and added, "Never mind, if I were you I wouldn't necessarily trust me, either. So is this guy still hanging around? What did he look like?"

Carrie shrugged helplessly. "It was dark, so I couldn't see him well. But he was tall, and big. Expensively dressed with too much jewelry. He had a thick French accent. Ring any bells?"

Jack thought hard, but no one in his past, not even the distant past, met such a description. He shook his head, puzzled. "I was about to dismiss what happened to my boat as a random prank, but now I'm not so sure . . . Carrie, I'm sorry you got caught in the middle of whatever this is."

Her eyes sparkled with mischief. "I'm not sorry. We have a real mystery on our hands." She lowered her voice to a melodramatic whisper. "Who is the wealthy but anonymous Frenchman, and why is he interested in Jack Harrington? And why is he terrorizing Carrie Bishop, an unsuspecting tourist from Des Moines who has unwittingly gotten herself caught up in a web of trickery and deceit—''

"Carrie, stop that!" Jack cut in. "This is not exciting, and we are not television detectives. This is my mystery, not yours. I don't want to be responsible for involving you in something when I don't have the faintest notion of what it's all about. Now if this French dude comes near you again, I want you to scream as loud as you can for the nearest cop. Got that?"

The amusement left Carrie's face. She leaned forward and whispered, "You mean I really *could* be in danger?"

Yes, he wanted to scream at her. His work was normally boring, at least to anyone but another historian or archaeologist, but if even a hint was breathed about the possibility of sunken treasure, his business became one of the most cutthroat and slimy in the world. He knew from personal experience. Apparently someone had breathed that hint. But who?

He wondered then if he should tell Carrie about the *Laurel*. If there was going to be any more nasty business he certainly didn't want her involved, but if for some reason she was in danger he wanted her to be prepared for it. He argued with himself for a moment, but in the end he decided not to confide in Carrie.

They lingered over dinner. Jack regaled Carrie with a few tales of his encounters with sharks and barracuda. Seemingly entranced, she listened to every word. He paused between stories to ask her about her job in Des Moines, her family and her friends, but she didn't seem eager to talk about herself.

"I'm afraid I don't have any exciting stories to match yours," she said, "unless you count the time the gift shop where I work was held up."

"You were held up at gunpoint?" Jack asked. "That's pretty hair-raising."

"No, not me. I was home sick with the flu that day, for which I am eternally grateful. But see what I mean? I'm afraid I've lived a pretty tame existence."

When the dinner had been stretched as long as was reasonable, Jack paid the check and escorted Carrie into the cool evening. He felt suddenly less talkative as he contemplated the unhappy prospect of putting an end to the evening. He couldn't remember when he'd enjoyed himself so much.

Silently they removed their shoes and began to retrace their steps up the beach. The tide was coming in, sending playful waves toward them.

Jack was once again assaulted with a feeling of intense longing as he watched Carrie scamper away from the encroaching water, laughing in delight. He wondered what it would be like to make love to her. He could see himself peeling that dress off her and taking those blasted pins out of her hair, though he knew such fantasies were way out of line. They'd met only hours ago, after all, and he could tell just by talking to her that she wasn't the type to go for what might appear to be a one-night stand.

Why did she hold such a fascination for him? Perhaps it was because he'd confided so much in her, more than he'd told anyone in a very long time. Maybe that explained why he felt so unaccountably close to her, and why he wanted to feel closer.

He was curious about her past, too, and what had prompted her to travel here alone. He wanted to know why she seemed to be grabbing for anything that promised excitement—including himself—and why at the same time she seemed so vulnerable.

Yes, he definitely wanted to know her better. But he knew he would simply whisk her to the hotel, kiss her on that impossible button nose and tell her goodbye. Period. For as much as he'd like to draw her into his life, and to enjoy a bit of her company while she was on St. Thomas, to do so might put her in more danger. He wouldn't do that, no matter how severely he was tempted.

Chapter Three

Carrie peered covertly at Jack as they walked up the beach in silence. She'd seen him angry and she'd seen him teasing, but this was the first time she'd seen him brooding. Was it something she'd done?

Upon further study of his handsome face, Carrie concluded that he wasn't upset, merely thoughtful. She decided not to disturb him, at least for a while. She had her own tangled thoughts to mull over, anyway—like how she'd felt on the dance floor, with Jack's arms around her and his hands moving over her back in tantalizing patterns. His touch, though feather light, had made her skin tingle and sting, but she soon forgot the sunburn in the delight his caresses brought. She wouldn't have dreamed of stopping him.

As they danced, all she could think about was how it would feel to have his hands on her bare flesh, what it would be like if there were no barrier between them, if they were dancing in the nude with their bodies touching from breast to thigh.... Her thoughts had made her blush then as now, and that was probably the first time she'd been thankful for a sunburn. Where did this sudden rush of . . . of *wantonness*, for lack of a better word, come from?

Carrie knew her usual way of thinking was rather conventional, but she had always believed that sex came after you fell in love and shared a meaningful, exclusive relationship with the man you married—or at least planned to marry.

But that was before she'd experienced the pure, white-hot desire that invaded her senses tonight. Married at nineteen and faithful to the same cold fish of a man for ten years, she hadn't allowed herself the luxury of even a moment's lust. She hadn't even understood the concept—until tonight.

She wanted Jack.

And why shouldn't she have him? After all, she was here to try new things, right? She shook her head and sighed. No, it wasn't right. She had no right to take him to bed for the sake of a new experience. The man was bound to have feelings, after all, and he might not appreciate being used any more than she would. And even if it didn't bother him, it would bother her.

Did he want her, too, she wondered? Yes, she knew he did, unless he was an awfully skillful actor. Was that why he was so quiet? Was he contemplating how to seduce the naive tourist from Des Moines? Or was he struggling with his conscience as to whether he should try to seduce her at all? She might seem to him an incredibly easy mark.

She hoped it was the latter. She liked the idea of Jack having a vigorous conscience and lots of scruples. Adventurous, brave and daring, but made of strong moral fiber. Yes, that was the image of Jack she wanted to save, to put in her mental scrapbook for those cold winter nights in Des Moines she would face when she left here.

They'd reached the stone staircase, and Jack sat on the bottom step to put on his socks and shoes while Carrie brushed the sand off the bottoms of her stockinged feet and slipped into her pumps. When she was done she came to stand beside him as he tied his laces. She laid one hand on top of his head and ran her fingers through the thick, black hair, as she'd wanted to do earlier that day. It would have been presumptuous then; it felt perfectly natural now.

He looked up, momentarily startled, then gave her a slow, lazy smile. "I've been miles away, haven't I?"

"It's okay. I'm glad you don't feel pressured to make witty conversation every minute. That means you're comfortable with me." She sat on the step next to him, unmindful now of mussing her white dress. It would wash.

Jack absently entwined his fingers in hers and gazed out at the moonlight reflected in the calm ocean. "Aren't you curious as to what I was thinking about?"

"A little. Do you want to talk about it?"

"Not really, but I feel I should." He tensed almost imperceptibly. "Please don't take this wrong. You're a very attractive, very, very desirable woman. Did I say very?"

She smiled as she nodded, despite the ominous tone of this conversation.

"But I think," he continued, "it would be a good idea if I took you back to your hotel and we said good night...and goodbye."

"Why?" she asked in a small voice. It was just a little rejection, she told herself. She could handle it.

"Because...because you were right earlier. I am involved in something—not something illegal, but apparently it is something dangerous. The sooner you disassociate yourself from me, the safer you'll be."

She took a deep breath and let it out slowly in a long, hopeless-sounding sigh. "You don't have to protect me,

Jack. I've had enough sheltering to last a lifetime. I grew up pampered and overprotected, and I married a wealthy doctor twenty years my senior who made every decision for me. For once I'd like someone to acknowledge the fact that I have a brain and that I know how to use it.''

''I'm sure you're an extremely intelligent woman,'' Jack agreed. He was tempted once again to tell her about the *Laurel*, but he refused to give in. He couldn't involve Carrie any further. But he had to state his case more firmly in order to convince her. ''Brains don't do you a heck of a lot of good against a knife or a gun. I won't be responsible for you. You'll have to seek your thrills with someone else.''

She stared at him, unbelieving for a moment. Why were men so obtuse sometimes? Hadn't she made it clear that she didn't want him to be responsible for her?

She extracted her hand from his, stood and brushed the sand from the back of her dress. ''Maybe you're right,'' she said, her calm voice a credit to her control. ''Maybe you *should* take me back to the hotel and we can forget we ever met. From now on I'll seek my thrills at the rumba contests.''

She turned and bolted up the stairs, but only made it up five or six steps before Jack caught up with her and placed a restraining hand on her arm. ''Carrie, wait a minute. I'm sorry about the thrill-seeking wisecrack. But try to see it from my point of view. I'd feel eternally guilty if something happened to you on account of me.''

Carrie swiped at an errant tear that had trickled down her cheek, feeling more than a little foolish. Why did her tears always show up at completely inappropriate times?

Jack had pegged her right, after all. She *was* thrill seeking, in a way. It wasn't that she wished to put herself in danger; she merely wanted a chance to get to know Jack, to explore the strange feelings he brought out in her. *That* was the thrill she wanted to experience. Was she wrong?

"Your apology is accepted," she said stiffly. They walked up the steps in silence, Carrie leading the way, until the dense foliage overhead obliterated what little moonlight there had been and she could no longer see the path in front of her. She stopped.

"What is it?" Jack asked.

"You'll have to lead the way. It's so dark I can't see."

He scooted past her. "Here, give me your hand." She let him guide her the rest of the way up the stairs, and by the time they reached the top, some of her confusion had quieted, only to be replaced with a sense of loss. She liked Jack Harrington. But he wanted her out of his life, and there wasn't a damn thing she could do about it.

As she clung to him during the ride home, she was less concerned that she would fall off the scooter and more aware of how nice it felt to hold him and how wonderful he smelled. She lamented the lovemaking that would never be between them, and she hoped that she would be able to say goodbye gracefully.

"Here we are, safe and sound," Jack said as he pulled up to a red curb by the hotel's front doors. He knew his cheerfulness sounded forced and he silently cursed the circumstances that had led to his uncomfortable moment. If only he'd met Carrie after this business with the *Laurel* was settled. If only he didn't *like* her so much. Under any other circumstances, they might have been able to give each other some beautiful times together and a healthy dose of affection.

Instead he was pushing away one of the nicest things to come his way in a long, long time.

At least she wasn't fuming at him anymore. She even smiled once as they made their way across the lobby and into the elevator.

They stopped in front of her door, and she fumbled nervously with the key as she attempted to fit it into the lock. Jack stilled her efforts by putting his hand over hers. She stopped struggling and looked up at him with enormous, blue-gray eyes that seemed to see straight into his soul.

"I wish this could have turned out differently, Carrie." His hand slid up her arm to her shoulder, her neck, then her cheek. He brushed the smooth skin there with his knuckles. "I don't blame you if you're put out with me, but I wish you'd overlook that long enough to give me a good-night kiss."

"I wouldn't dream of denying myself." Her purse and her keys dropped to the floor. She took half a step closer to him, and her arms snaked their way around his neck as he drew her body against his. He lowered his head until his mouth hovered mere centimeters from hers. She pulled him the rest of the way, and he thought he would melt from the sheer sweetness of that first touch of her lips.

They were dewy soft, offering Jack a unique taste that was Carrie's own special flavor. He kept the kiss gentle, letting his lips move slowly over hers, resisting the urge to thrust his tongue into her sweet, inviting mouth. He did, however, give in to one temptation that had been tormenting him all evening. He reached up and pulled the jeweled comb out of her hair, expecting the silky gold tresses to tumble down to her shoulders. They didn't.

"You've watched too many kisses on TV," Carrie murmured against Jack's mouth. She reached up and pulled four or five pins out of the chignon and gave her head a shake. And at last the shimmering waves of gold were free.

Jack buried his face in her hair and breathed in the green-apple scent. "You're beautiful, Carrie," he whispered. "I hope you'll remember this evening fondly." He handed her the comb and gave her one final kiss on the forehead before letting go of her and turning away. With all the calm he could muster, he walked toward the elevator, barely resisting the urge to turn and look at her one last time. He heard the key go into the lock, heard the door open, then shut.

The elevator doors were just beginning to close when Jack heard the scream.

He nearly dislocated his shoulder as he shoved his way out through the closing elevator doors. He sprinted to Carrie's door. It was locked. He banged on it and called her name. Finally it opened, and Carrie fell breathless into his arms, her face a mask of sheer terror.

"Oh, Jack, I'm so glad you came back. Someone's been in my room. Look..."

Jack stroked Carrie's hair and held her trembling body close as he surveyed the damage to the room. Her possessions had been strewn all over the floor. A bottle of rum had been opened and poured over the carpet. The bedspread sported a five-foot-long tear, as if someone had ripped through it with a knife. Jack's hackles rose at the symbolic brutality.

He sat Carrie down in a chair and went to check the bathroom. Her cosmetic bag had been emptied onto the floor, and broken glass from the mirror of a compact littered the area at his feet, along with crumbled bits of broken eye shadow and blusher.

When he returned to the main room he found Carrie holding the broken pieces of her plastic pirate's ship, looking quite forlorn. "It was for my nephew, Josh."

"I'm sorry. This is all my—"

"Why the pointless destruction?" she continued, her voice suddenly sharp and angry. "What does the person who did this want from me? There was nothing of real value here, so the vandal went out of his way to destroy stuff that didn't mean anything to anyone except me...." Her words trailed off.

Lord, she looked pale under that sunburn, Jack thought. In fact, he was sure she was going to pass out. He took the now unrecognizable pieces of the model from her hands and laid them on the dresser, then encouraged her to put her head in her lap. "Slow deep breaths. That's right."

After a minute or so she raised her head. The color had returned to her face, but her eyes were still shiny with unshed tears.

Without words Jack drew her out of the chair and sat her on the bed, well away from the slashed area, piling pillows behind her for support. She let him guide her through the movements without protest. He removed her shoes, wrapped the edge of the bedspread over her legs, then sat beside her and held her hand. The threat of her tears subsided, and he could hear her breathing slow down as she absorbed his relative calm.

"I'm okay now," she said. "Sorry about that. I faint at the drop of a hat, so it's nothing to worry about."

"Hey, you did just fine. It's a perfectly natural reaction to be upset when your privacy has been violated. I'm just glad you weren't here when..." He refused to verbalize the rest.

Jack considered what to do next. The person behind this vandalism should know by now that Carrie wasn't involved in Jack's affairs, that she was just a tourist. One look at those tourist-trap souvenirs would have tipped him off. Whoever the culprit was, he was trying to get at Jack through Carrie—and doing a pretty good job, too.

"Whoever did this understands the power of intimidation," he said aloud. "We can't let it get to us, Carrie, if we want to stay in the game. We can't let him scare us."

"But Jack, I *am* scared. And I don't even know what game we're playing! You were right, this isn't exciting. This is the pits."

It was time he told Carrie the truth. He hadn't wanted to involve her, but she was involved now whether he liked it or not. She'd been chosen as a target by someone who knew Jack would be a sucker for this kind of tactic. And if he abandoned her now he couldn't be sure she'd be out of danger. He would have to bring Carrie into his confidence and keep her close—that or get her off the island. And even if he asked her to leave, he doubted she would agree.

"I'm sorry about your pirate ship," he said. "Could I make up for the loss if I showed you a real sunken ship, and maybe a little bit of treasure?"

Carrie perked up immediately. "Is that what this is all about? You've found a sunken treasure ship of some kind? How exciting! I...I mean, how interesting," she amended.

"I'm not sure what I've found," said Jack, moving closer to her and slipping an arm around her shoulders. "But I was poking around a reef off St. John. There's a wreck there, a little British steamer called the *Laurel* that crashed into the reef during a storm around the turn of the century. It's believed to be a mail packet, and long ago it was picked clean of anything remotely valuable. It broke apart on the ocean floor, and I doubt anyone has even looked at the site for decades."

"Why are you interested in it?" Carrie asked.

"There was a hurricane here last spring, right after I came to St. Thomas. Hurricanes have a way of stirring up the ocean bottom, and sometimes new things will turn up on old wrecks. I happened to be in the area of the *Laurel*, testing some new equipment, and something did turn up.''

''What did you find?'' Carrie asked, almost breathless with anticipation.

''An eight-escudo piece.''

''A what?''

''A gold doubloon—an old coin—dated 1749. I also found part of a coral rosary with a gold cross.''

Carrie sat up and tucked her legs under her, a thoughtful expression on her face. She seemed to have recovered from the shock. At least Jack was thankful for that. ''That's strange stuff for a British mail ship to be carrying, especially a rosary. Precious few Englishmen carried those at the turn of the century.''

''Exactly. Hey, how do you know so much?''

''I was a history major,'' she answered, dismissing the fact with a wave of her hand. ''So go on, what happened next?''

''Not much, really. I've spent the past two weeks diving near the wreck site. So far nothing terribly interesting has turned up, but I have a lot of ground to cover.''

''And you think someone sabotaged your boat to prevent you from diving on the *Laurel*, so they can have a chance to dive there and find the treasure before you,'' Carrie concluded. ''That's perfectly awful.''

''Nonetheless, people do that sort of thing—and worse—when they smell gold. The funny thing is, I haven't told anyone about this. No one could know about what I found.''

''Maybe someone's spying on you,'' Carrie suggested. ''If you've been diving in the same spot for two weeks, they might suspect something.''

He shrugged. ''It's possible, I suppose.''

''What if this unprincipled person *does* beat you to a treasure? What can you do about it?''

"It's not going to happen in the next few days, unless a miracle occurs. That wreck is spread over several acres of ocean floor, and the actual area I'm exploring is at least a hundred yards from the main site. I've been careful not to anchor the boat in exactly the same place every time, so no one could pinpoint the location I'm surveying. In answer to your question, though, there isn't much I can do about it. You can't file a claim here. It's first come, first serve."

"Then you have to stop this person. He's already broken the law. If we find out who it is we can have him thrown in jail."

Jack had to smile at Carrie's naivete. "It's not so easy to get someone thrown in jail and keep him there. But you're right about one thing. We have to find out who our culprit is."

She pounced on his comment like a hungry cat on a slow mouse. "*Our* culprit? Does that mean you're going to let me share *your* mystery?"

He sighed. "I don't have any choice. It was your room they ransacked, after all."

"Thank you, Jack," she said with a dignified nod of her head. Then the merry lights returned to her eyes and she gave a teasing smile.

Even if she fully appreciated the danger, Jack realized, she still thought this was exciting, and her romanticism just might get her in trouble.

"Look, Carrie, I want you to know exactly what you might be getting into. I played this game once before and I lost—big time."

"You mean you've actually found sunken treasure before?"

He nodded, mentally bracing himself to relive the incident he'd so carefully avoided discussing for six years. "I chased that Spanish galleon for almost a decade. Got wind of her when I was in college, wrote a master's thesis on her. The more I studied, the more I became convinced that the *San Pedro Y Santa Maria* and her treasure lay hidden in the Florida Keys. I even went to Spain to study documents in the archives of Seville. And I spent every waking hour reading or scouring the ocean floor.''

"And?" Carrie leaned forward.

"I found her. I filed an exclusive lease to the area. And I entered into a partnership with a professional salvager named Charlie Hill..." Just the mention of the man's name made Jack's gut twist. He paused to take two deep breaths before continuing. "Charlie pulled a fast one on me. I'm not sure how he did it, but I think he had a friend in the government who falsified some documents for him. At any rate, suddenly Charlie owned the lease and I was a poacher."

"Couldn't you do anything? Did you go to the authorities? Did you—"

"I tried everything. I went to the authorities. I went to the newspapers. I even appealed to the governor. But apparently Charlie Hill had friends in high places. I got sued, arrested and barraged with bad publicity. I even got shot at. Anyway, my lawyer persuaded everyone to drop their charges if I got the hell out of Florida. Which I did. So you see, this is no tame game."

Carrie was silent for a time, giving Jack the chance to get a handle on his barely controlled anger. He shouldn't be carrying around this bitterness, not after six years. Maybe it was good he'd brought it out in the open.

"Did Charlie Hill get rich?" she finally asked.

"Very. I think what makes me the angriest, though, is the fact that he pulled stuff out of the water without the slightest reverence for its historical value. He destroyed artifacts in his haste to find gold. He...he desecrated the whole site."

She squeezed his hand, offering her silent, eloquent understanding—just what he needed at the moment.

"So what's our next step?" she asked, briskly changing the subject.

"I think we should alert hotel security to the fact they've been remiss in their duties and have them move you to another room. And while they're doing that, I think I should take you to the restaurant downstairs for a stiff drink."

"My feelings exactly. I'll buy."

Jack paused when they'd exited the room, dropping to one knee and peering intently at the doorknob and the edge of the oak door. "Hmm."

"What?" Carrie asked.

"There's no sign of a forced entry. I wonder if our vandal has a key to your room?"

Carrie shivered. "I haven't let my room key out of my sight since I got here."

"He could have gotten a passkey, I suppose. I'm sure dozens of people have access to them." That thought didn't comfort him. If the vandal did have a passkey, moving her to another room wouldn't be much safer.

When Jack and Carrie stepped off the elevator into the lobby, the first person they saw was Myra, decked out like a flamingo, complete with a pink feather in her hair. She was sitting behind her desk, leafing dejectedly through a stack of files.

"What happened to your hot date with the rich yachtsman?" Jack asked as they paused in Myra's corner of the lobby.

"Oh, you mean Claude? He came to pick me up, we had one drink in the lounge, then suddenly he got called away on business. Some hot date. You two are hitting it off, I see. Are you heading for the rumba contest?"

This last comment wasn't without a touch of sarcasm, Jack noted.

"Just a drink and maybe some coffee. You want to join us?"

"No, I think I'll mope in solitude while I get caught up on this busy work."

They bid her goodbye and headed for the night manager's desk. When Carrie told the manager her tale, he was horrified.

"Of course, we'll move you to another room right away. And we'll clean up the mess and reimburse you for any damages, Ms. Bishop. I'm so sorry. We'll have security get on the case right away."

"We'll be in the restaurant," Jack added as the man picked up the phone and dialed security. "You can call us when the new room is ready."

"I should go pack my things," Carrie said as Jack took her elbow and led her toward the coffee shop.

"They'll take care of it. You can count on the hotel bending over backward the next few days to make sure you're safe and happy."

By the time they were seated in the lounge, Carrie had changed her mind about the drink, opting for hot tea instead. The security director, dragged out of bed from the looks of him, approached them at their table a short time later and gently questioned Carrie about the vandalism. She revealed nothing about the other strange events surrounding her that day, having agreed with Jack beforehand not to bring up the sabotage to his boat or the incident with the Frenchman.

In a few minutes a bellman came to the table, handed Carrie a key and gave her directions to her new room. Soon she and Jack were once again standing in front of her door.

With all the adrenaline in their systems, Jack didn't trust himself to kiss her again. So he gave her a not-so-brotherly hug instead.

"Sleep well, Carrie. I'll see you tomorrow."

"Wait, Jack. How can I get in touch with you?"

"I won't be far. Until this mess is cleared up, or until you're safely back in Des Moines, you've got yourself a bodyguard. Is that okay?"

She gave Jack a sunny smile that warmed him to his bones. "That's just fine. Good night, Jack."

Carrie awoke with a sense of anticipation and optimism that surprised her, given last night's terrifying incident. This was turning out to be the strangest vacation, but it surely was one she'd never forget. As she stood in the hot shower, she wondered what her friends at work would think about her adventure. Of course, they'd all tried to talk her out of coming on this vacation....

"Carrie Bishop, you don't know the first thing about traveling..."

"Why, you've never even been out of the Midwest..."

"It's so dangerous going by yourself..."

How would they react when she described Jack and how he'd thought she was a saboteur, and how a mysterious, nameless Frenchman had interrogated her in a bathroom hallway, and how her room had been broken into? The answers to those questions were easy. Dear though they were, those conservative little volunteers who worked for her at the hospital gift shop wouldn't see the drama or the excitement of her adventure—or the romance, for that matter. In fact, they would have only one thing to say to her: "We told you so."

Ah, well, let them lecture, Carrie thought. Or maybe she wouldn't tell them at all.

A piece of white paper on the maroon carpet caught her eye as she dressed. It hadn't been there when she'd gone to take her shower, she was sure. She walked over to it, stared at it suspiciously for a few moments, then gingerly picked it up. Fumbling with clumsy fingers she opened it, and a rush of relief swept over her. It was from Jack.

> Dear Carrie:
> I know I'm a negligent bodyguard, but I had to take care of some business this morning. I arranged for Myra to keep you company until I come back. She's waiting for you in the lobby. Please, *please* don't wander off anywhere by yourself.

It was signed simply, "Jack."

The message warmed her. He really was concerned for her safety, and just for that she'd do as he asked. The idea of wasting her morning in the hotel lobby rankled her slightly, but perhaps she could make use of the time.

She found Myra in the lobby a few minutes later. The tour director was surrounded by the babbling members of a large group that had arrived the night before, all trying to sign up for glass-bottom boat expeditions, snorkel classes and catamaran cruises. Carrie smiled behind her hand and took an out-of-the-way chair to wait as Myra handled the tourists with her usual aplomb.

"One at a time," she said firmly but pleasantly for at least the fifth time since Carrie had arrived on the scene. "Here are your tickets for a complementary rum punch at the welcome cocktail party this evening... No, I'm sorry, we've had to cancel the scuba classes for today. Perhaps tomorrow... The tennis courts are on level three on the south side. If you'll all consult your maps..."

Were all tourists as pushy and dull-witted as this particular group seemed to be? Carrie wondered. Did Myra and Jack lump her in the same category? She shuddered, hoping that she appeared to have at least a little more dignity than the average tourist.

"Whew!" Myra looked over at Carrie and wiped her brow with an exaggerated gesture as the last of the yammering group ambled away. She motioned for Carrie to move into a chair closer to the desk. "Good morning. It's nice to see a friendly face. I understand I'm your substitute bodyguard this morning."

Carrie nodded. "Did Jack tell you what happened?"

"I heard two of the security guards talking about it this morning, but I didn't know it was your room until I talked to Jack. I'm so sorry your first visit with us had to be spoiled that way. I've worked here for more than five years and I've never heard of such a thing happening before."

"Nothing like this has ever happened to *me* before," Carrie added. "I don't know what I would have done if Jack hadn't been there to calm me down. But I don't intend to let it spoil my vacation. What do we have lined up for today, anyway—deep sea fishing?"

"I, uh, canceled your reservations. Jack said to keep you here." This last was said with some embarrassment.

"Jack said! Who does he think he—" Carrie clamped her mouth shut. She could be miffed that Jack had passed her along to Myra like a troublesome parcel and that he was getting a little high-handed with throwing orders around, but she had to remind herself that he was doing these things because he was worried for her safety. And perhaps he was justifiably concerned.

"I must say, he is acting strangely," said Myra, idly doodling on the edge of a sign-up sheet. "If I didn't know better, I'd guess he has a case for you. I mean, there's really no reason for him to be guarding you like a china doll. The vandalism couldn't have been aimed at you personally. The boys in security think your room was a random choice."

"Why do you say, 'If I didn't know better'?" Carrie's dander was up now. "Is it so unusual that he might want to spend time with me?"

Myra placed a reassuring hand on Carrie's arm, looking genuinely contrite. "Oh, sugar, I didn't mean it to sound that way. It's just that, well, as long as I've known Jack he hasn't shown the slightest interest in a woman—despite the fact that they're constantly falling at his feet. I've always thought it a shame that all that charm and those good looks were wasted on a man who was so preoccupied with his work he had no time for play."

Carrie nodded, hoping Myra would go on without prompting. She was proving to be a valuable source of information.

"Yes, he's a charmer all right," Myra continued, shaking her head and staring wistfully into space, and Carrie suspected that Myra hoarded a spark of desire for Jack herself. But then Myra turned and, all business once again, she shook a finger at Carrie. "You mark my words, Miss Bishop. Jack has one interest and one interest only, and that's his damned treasure hunting. Don't you lose your heart to him or you'll be hurt, as sure as I'm sitting here."

Carrie responded with a deceptively carefree smile and a short laugh. "Oh, please, how could I possibly get hurt? I won't be here long enough to fall in love."

Chapter Four

Jack ran his hand over the hull of his boat at the place where the hole had been. The patch was barely visible underwater, even at close range. He couldn't feel the seams. The patch was holding, even after the *Carrie* had cruised at high speed for several minutes.

He surfaced and pulled off his mask, then waved at the stout man who waited for him on the dock. "Looks good," he called as he kicked slowly toward the landing. "I can't believe you did it so quickly."

"I used that new fiberglass repair stuff. It dries almost instantly. And I worked overtime, too. I always take care of my customers who pay on time." The stout man guffawed loudly for no particular reason as he stuck out his hand to help Jack out of the water and onto the pier. Then he lowered his voice. "Hey, you got someone waiting for you. Pretty little gal."

Jack's eyes immediately scanned the area in and around Dave's Dry Dock and Marina until he spied her, sitting primly on a cast-iron chair, decked out in a white sailor blouse and matching walking shorts.

Carrie looked up just then and Jack smiled and waved. He settled quickly with Dave, dashing off a check right there on the dock. He stuffed his mask, snorkel and fins into his duffel and gave in happily to the irresistible force drawing him toward Carrie.

"So, how did your morning go?" he asked, tweaking her ponytail and pulling up a chair beside her.

"Bo-ring, thanks to you. I didn't come to the Virgin Islands to sit in a hotel lobby." But she spoiled the admonishment with a grin. "Actually I had fun. I ate a breakfast grand enough to put me into a happy stupor, then I played bingo by the pool and actually won a scarf. But I am gratified to be liberated."

"I hope Myra didn't mind driving you over here."

"She didn't, but she says you owe her a fresh lobster next time you run across one. How's the boat?"

"Good as new. And we're going to try her out right now. Did you bring your suit?"

Carrie nodded. "But I'm not sure I should be in the sun so soon."

"You won't be," Jack said as he stood and picked up her tote bag. They walked toward the boat, where Dave was loading nine gleaming air tanks into a storage rack. "We'll be underwater most of the time."

"Underwater?" Carrie shook her head. "Uh-uh, not me. I told you I was chicken."

"There is nothing to be afraid of."

"What about all those shark stories you told me last night? And the barracuda?"

"None of those things happened in the Virgin Islands. All the sharks here are friendly, I promise."

"Friendly sharks? That's a contradiction in terms."

Dave had finished loading the tanks. He shook hands with Jack then scurried off to take care of a boat that had pulled up to the gas pump.

Despite her apprehension at the prospect of scuba diving, Carrie managed to relax and enjoy their cruise to St. John. Jack had bought some groceries earlier that morning, and once the course was set he busied himself making hearty chicken salad sandwiches. They sat in the shade of the awning over the bridge high atop the *Carrie* and enjoyed the sandwiches, some fresh papaya and a few sips of crisp white wine.

Jack skirted the more heavily trafficked areas around Cruz Bay and traveled along the southern shore until he arrived at a charming cove, where the calm turquoise ocean met a sheltered strip of sugar-white sand. The cove was utterly deserted. He maneuvered the boat into the shallows, cut the motor and dropped anchor.

He handed Carrie a bottle of waterproof sunscreen. "Put some of this on your shoulders. That should protect you until we go under."

Carrie's nerves came vigorously to life. "I don't think I can go through with it, Jack."

"I promise you, you can," he insisted. "We'll ease into it, and I won't make you do anything you don't want to."

His words were warm and reassuring. Carrie inhaled and exhaled slowly to calm her racing pulse as she removed her outer clothing, revealing a modest white one-piece underneath, and applied the sunscreen. All the while she watched Jack assemble an intimidating array of equipment: masks, tanks, flippers, vests of some kind, even an underwater camera. Hoses and tubes protruded from everything, with complicated-looking gauges attached.

"Why don't you jump in and paddle around a bit to get used to it?" Jack suggested. "Have you ever been swimming in salt water?"

Carrie shook her head, her front teeth worrying her lower lip.

"You'll be pleasantly surprised. Go ahead, jump in."

Chicken, she berated herself. Did she really think Jack would let her drown? Sending up a silent prayer she held her breath and launched herself from the diving platform in back of the boat.

The water was cool and invigorating. Other than that, the first thing Carrie noticed was that she floated to the surface like a cork. With very little effort she could keep her head above water. She experimented with several floating positions, then turned a somersault.

"How's it feel?" Jack called to her.

She looked up and saw that he was in the process of strapping a tank to his back. "It feels fine," she answered.

"Good. Swim over here and get some flippers and a mask."

She did, following Jack's patient instructions for putting on the equipment.

Soon, to her immense surprise, she was zipping around with astounding speed and agility, looking at the sandy bottom through the mask. The water was crystal clear, revealing the subaqueous scene in unbelievably sharp detail.

"A fish! Jack, I saw a fish down there!"

She heard him laughing. "You'll see lots of fish before we're through. Head for the beach, I'm right behind you."

Gentle waves lapped at their knees as Jack explained the functioning of each piece of equipment, then showed her how to strap on a tank. Carrie shivered inwardly each time Jack's fingers brushed against her bare skin while he adjusted the various straps. Her hands itched to touch him in return, though Jack obviously needed no help with his equipment. Her excitement at the prospect of this new experience only heightened her awareness of Jack as a man, and she had to remind herself often to listen to his instructions rather than watch the muscle play of his arms and chest.

Carrie's anxiety returned when she submerged herself completely. She couldn't breathe! Then she realized she was holding her breath. She took a couple of tentative gasps before convincing herself that the regulator would indeed supply her with adequate oxygen.

Jack led her through several swimming exercises. He showed her how to clear her mask of water, then showed her some basic hand signals so they would be able to communicate below the surface.

The final exercise was the most intimidating—learning how to "buddy breathe" in the unlikely event that one of them lost their air supply during a dive. At a depth of about twenty-five feet Jack pulled the regulator out of his mouth and, with comically urgent hand signals, begged Carrie to share her oxygen with him.

She obliged, though her stomach turned flip-flops for the few seconds she was forced to go without breathing. Jack returned the regulator, and she took a couple of frantic breaths of her own before calming down. They traded the regulator back and forth several times before making a slow ascent to the surface.

"You did it!" Jack congratulated Carrie when they broke through the surface of the water. "Were you scared?"

"Terrified," Carrie admitted as she pulled her mask over her forehead.

"Come on, let's swim back to the boat," he said. "You're ready for a real dive."

"But I like it here," she objected, her nerves returning to haunt her once again. "It's calm and safe—and shallow."

"Come on, chicken, follow me. Have I steered you wrong yet?"

Climbing on board with two tons of hardware attached to her body wasn't nearly as easy as getting in had been. She clung to Jack, relying on his strength as he helped her into the boat, then fell in an exhausted heap on the deck. Jack loosened the straps that held her tank in place, and she slipped out of them gratefully.

"You did very well, you know," he said.

Carrie smiled triumphantly. "I did, didn't I? Imagine that."

"You're not still scared, are you?"

She shook her head, thinking more about the reassuring hand Jack had placed on her shoulder than the actual question.

"Good." Jack's hand moved from her shoulder to gently cup her jaw. He swiftly captured her lips in a kiss that was as unexpected as it was exhilarating. Carrie was still reeling with the aftereffects when the boat's engine rumbled to life.

The next time Jack cut the engine, the sea was not nearly so calm. They were anchored off a point at the southeastern tip of St. John, directly over the main wreck site, Jack told Carrie. They would submerge, then swim about a hundred yards to the east, where he had discovered the artifacts.

"Before we dive, I should explain more about the *Laurel* and exactly what it is we might be looking for," he said. With a detailed map in front of them, he illustrated where the English mail packet had crashed into the reef and broken apart during a storm in 1899.

"Right there is where I found the coin, and there the rosary," he said. "This grouping of round rocks, which were used for ballast, indicates that the ship was struck—'' he pulled out another diagram, a cutaway drawing of an old ship ''—from this direction, and the current carried it—'' again he switched to the map ''—here. I'm guessing that whatever was in the *Laurel*'s hold spilled out long before she sank. That's why it wasn't found before.''

''How do you know the name of the ship?'' Carrie asked.

''From old newspapers and magazines. They were especially keen on shipwrecks around here, and they tended to report on them in great detail. There's also a local man, a good friend of mine named Gifford, who used to do a lot of diving. He confirmed the existence of the ship. He told me it was picked clean even before he was born—and he's in his seventies.''

''So what else do you know about it?'' Carrie asked, her interest growing.

''Only one crewman survived the wreck. He tried to get a salvage party together, but unfortunately, he died a few days later. That's about all that was written in the papers.''

Carrie studied the diagram of the old vessel. ''Is there anything left of the ship?'' she asked, picturing the ghostly remains of a wooden hull.

''There's nothing at all left of the timbers. They were eaten by worms long ago. In fact, you won't be able to tell there was a shipwreck here at all. Most anything that was left is encrusted with coral by now and very hard to identify. But if we look sharp we might get lucky. Search among the coral for funny-looking clumps, straight edges, right angles.''

''Can I look at the fish first?'' she asked.

Jack laughed. ''Yes, by all means, look at the fish. And look for a lobster for Myra. Shall we?''

Carrie's eyes swept the area as she donned her gear once again. The wind whipped the ocean against outcroppings of rock with frightening intensity.

"We'll be dashed to bits," she mumbled, not really intending Jack to hear, but he did.

"You'll be surprised at how much calmer it is a few feet down," he reassured her. "How much air do you have left in your tank?"

Carrie consulted the gauge. "It says forty-five minutes."

"That should be plenty. Keep an eye on it. Do you remember what to do when the needle reaches the red area?"

"I point to the gauge and then up," Carrie answered.

The last thing Jack gave Carrie before they submerged was a mesh bag to loop over her shoulder. "For any goodies you might find. But don't get your hopes up. Like I told you last night, I haven't found anything in a couple of weeks."

Carrie forgot all about the shipwreck as soon as she discovered the reef. She'd seen pictures and she'd watched Jacques Cousteau on television, but nothing had prepared her for the elemental beauty of the reef and its inhabitants. It was as if she'd been dropped into a tropical fish tank. Coral in every describable color and shape grew to staggering proportions, in long, slender branches, broad, lacy fans and enormous, Technicolor spheres. The living wall dropped off dramatically to what looked like a hundred feet down.

A school of small, bright yellow fish scattered before Carrie as she swam toward them. She encountered other fish of neon blue, red, orange and black in varying shapes and sizes. A pair of what looked like angelfish eyed her curiously as they passed.

She glanced at Jack, who swam beside her, and gave him a thumbs up sign.

Jack allowed her to goggle at the fish a while longer, then motioned for her to follow him across the top of the reef and down again, to a sandy area where the reef thinned out. He pointed to a scattering of round rocks—some of the ballast rocks he'd mentioned earlier, she presumed. They swam a little farther, until he stopped and instructed her with hand signals that this was the area he had chosen for them to search.

He handed her a paddle and showed her how to fan the sand in order to delve deeper. Then he left her on her own, working an area several feet away.

Carrie enjoyed herself. This was something like an Easter egg hunt, she decided, only she didn't know what the eggs looked like. She saw a fist-sized chunk of dead coral and picked it up, examining it for suspicious shapes, straight edges or corners, as Jack had instructed. Seeing nothing remarkable about it she discarded it, only to pick up another and repeat the process. She used her paddle to dislodge a third piece, and when she pulled it loose from the sand, another piece came with it.

It was this fourth piece that captured her attention. It was smaller than a tennis ball, and it looked different from the others. She couldn't say precisely why, even upon studying it, but she stuck it in her net bag, anyway.

A movement caught her eye, and she turned swiftly, thoughts of moray eels and poisonous sea snakes suddenly coming to mind. Then she saw what had moved. A lobster was hiding in the rocks, with just his antennae protruding.

Carrie wasn't about to tackle it on her own. She started to move in Jack's direction, intending to get his help, when she noticed a strange sensation, a light-headedness that made her dizzy and caused her to see spots before her eyes. She inhaled deeply, then again, only to have the sensation intensify.

Something was wrong with her tank.

She glanced at her air gauge, which said she still had a good twenty minutes left. But breathing was becoming more difficult with every passing second.

Jack. She had to get to Jack. She waved at him, but he was busy studying something and didn't see her. Determinedly, she began kicking her flippered feet in his direction.

It seemed like minutes, but it must have been only a few seconds before she reached him. She grabbed onto his arm and, when she had his undivided attention, promptly forgot every hand signal she'd learned except one. She pointed to her gauge and then up toward the surface.

He looked at her gauge, pointed to his watch and gave her the okay signal.

She shook her head. What was the signal for trouble? She couldn't think! Finally she pulled the regulator out of her mouth and pushed the air-release button. When no bubbles came pouring out of the mouthpiece, Jack finally understood. Even as his eyes registered shock and concern he was jerking his regulator out of his mouth and pushing it into hers.

Carrie took four deep, slow breaths, remembering not to hyperventilate. The light-headedness vanished, the spots disappeared. She handed the regulator back to Jack, mouthing a relieved "Thank you."

Jack brought them to the surface gradually. They shared his air, just as they'd shared hers in practice. A sense of calm stole over Carrie. She knew now everything would be all right.

When they broke through the surface, Carrie took in great gulps of the fresh air. She'd never dreamed that simply breathing could be so joyful.

"Carrie, are you okay?" Jack couldn't remember being so scared since the time he'd been shot at in Florida.

Carrie nodded and managed a weak smile.

"Are you sure? Here, you can rest against me for a minute." He took her hand and brought it to rest on his shoulder. She sagged against him for a few seconds, then pulled away.

"No, I'm all right. Oh, Jack, I'm so sorry. I forgot all my hand signals. I really panicked—"

"Sorry?" Jack had to laugh. "Carrie, darling, you were nothing short of marvelous. I don't know anyone who could have gone through what you just did so calmly. How long were you out of air?"

Carrie shrugged. "It thinned out a little before I realized something was wrong. But then I was pretty dizzy—oh, look how far away the boat is. How do we get back?"

"Same way we got here, but on top of the water this time." He helped her fit her mask and snorkel into place, and with slow, measured strokes they made their way to the boat. Jack's thoughts churned all the while. What had happened to Carrie's air supply? He'd filled hundreds of tanks at Dave's marina since coming to the Virgin Islands. Nothing like this had ever happened to him—not here, not anywhere.

There was only one answer, and Jack didn't like it a bit. Someone had tampered with Carrie's tank.

Wrapped in a large towel and sipping a calming glass of wine, Carrie watched Jack thoughtfully as he pushed his boat at full throttle toward Dave's marina. She didn't like seeing him silent and brooding like this—not when that muscle in his jaw was ticking, indicating the anger that lay just below the surface.

She knew he wasn't angry at her. In fact, he'd been all kindness and concern when they'd returned to the boat, making sure she was warm and dry and that she had suffered no long-term ill effects from her brush with suffocation. But once she'd assured him she was fine, he'd grown quiet and ominously thoughtful.

He'd tested his eight remaining air tanks and discovered that four of them suffered from the same malady as Carrie's tank. With the exception of a string of wildly colorful curses, he'd remained silent since then.

They pulled up to the pier. Jack wasted little time securing the boat, then strode purposefully toward Dave, who was just waving goodbye to another customer.

The smile faded from the affable Dave's face when Jack told him of the near-disaster. "Carrie could have been killed," Jack said succinctly, his feet planted firmly on the dock and his fists clenched in a stance of barely contained fury. "I want to know what happened to those tanks."

"I just don't know," said Dave, wringing his chubby hands and shaking his balding head. "I've never...I mean, could something be wrong with my equipment? Thank goodness I haven't filled any other tanks today."

Jack and Carrie followed him inside. Carrie put her hand on Jack's arm in a soothing gesture, and when he looked at her she shook her head. "Don't go so hard on Dave," she whispered. "I'm sure it's not his fault."

The angry line on Jack's face softened a bit, and he nodded.

Together, Jack and Dave inspected the equipment in the back room where Dave filled scuba tanks. Carrie busied herself by examining the mind-boggling array of boating paraphernalia crammed into every corner and covering every wall of Dave's Dry Dock and Marina, all the while training her ear to the conversation in the back room. She already knew they would find nothing. It was apparent that someone had deliberately sabotaged Jack's tanks and no one else's, though she supposed it was prudent to rule out other possibilities first.

"Was anyone strange hanging around here today?" Jack asked as the two men emerged from the back room. Jack's animosity toward Dave had evaporated, replaced by a look of grim determination.

Dave's round face scrunched up in an expression of concentration. "Let's see, it was a busy morning, but I knew most of the folks who came in. Except for that one guy—" Dave smiled and shook his head. "He doesn't seem like the type that would be tampering with air tanks just for kicks. He's a rich fellow, not from around here—"

"Who was he?" Carrie and Jack asked together.

"I don't rightly remember the name. He was French, or maybe Canadian."

Jack and Carrie looked at each other, then at Dave. "That's who we're looking for," Jack said. "Are you sure you can't remember his name?"

"No, but I can show you his yacht." Dave led them outside, walking to the end of the dock where Charlotte Amalie's harbor was visible in every direction. "He sailed in on that nice one right out..." Dave scanned the harbor. "That's funny."

"What?" Jack and Carrie said, again together.

"It's gone."

After a few moments of frustrated silence, Carrie asked, "What was he doing here? Did he buy something?"

"Yeah," Dave answered, "he bought some gas for his launch."

"Did he pay with a credit card?"

Light dawned in Dave's eyes. "Sure! I got the receipt in here!"

Once again the three went inside. Dave flipped through his day's receipts, finally producing the one signed by the wealthy Frenchman. Three heads bent over the receipt. The card imprint was smeared and the signature was scrawled, but the first name, at least, was legible: Claude.

Carrie looked at Jack. "Know anyone named Claude?"

Jack shook his head. "No. How about you?"

"No, but the name does sound familiar. I've heard it recently, somewhere... Wait, I know!"

Jack was already nodding his understanding. "Myra's new boyfriend. She said he was a rich European with a yacht. It has to be the same guy."

They thanked Dave, who was still apologizing profusely for the mishap, and once again boarded the *Carrie*.

"What are we going to say to Myra?" Carrie asked as Jack headed the boat toward the hotel. "We can't just go up to her and say, 'Hey, Myra, your boyfriend's a crook and a thug.'"

"The hell we can't. How do you think this Claude person got into your room? He had to have swiped a passkey from Myra. And how do you suppose he knew where to find us last night? Myra told him. He's been pumping her for information about us for two days, and Myra's been spoon-feeding it to him. She's got a mouth bigger than—" His voice dropped. "Ah, Carrie, I'm sorry. I've really let my temper get away from me today. But when I think what could have happened—"

"It didn't happen, Jack," she said softly. "No one was hurt, at least not this time. You're letting him get to you with these cheap tricks."

Jack pursed his lips and nodded. Then he held out his hand to her. "Come here. I want you close to me. I want to hold on to you, make sure you don't go anywhere."

She let him pull her onto the seat next to him. Yes, this was what she wanted, too. Though she'd put on a brave front, the harrowing experience this afternoon had terrified her and left her quaking like gelatin inside. She'd longed for the security of Jack's strong arm around her, and now he was obliging her. She nestled comfortably against his hard chest and imagined herself absorbing his strength, his courage. She inhaled deeply of the salty scent of male skin bathed in seawater, feeling quite at home.

"I don't ever want to be scared like that again," he said softly, his breath tickling the top of her head.

"Believe me, neither do I," she murmured. She felt a reassuring squeeze, then a feather-light touch against her cheek as Jack smoothed away an unruly strand of her blond hair. His hand lingered. His fingers ran lightly over her ear, tracing its shell-like curve.

Carrie felt compelled to tilt her face and look into Jack's eyes. She saw desire there and felt an answering thrum of longing in her own heart.

His fingers traced a path along her jawline. Gently he tilted her chin higher still, making her lips accessible to his. His mouth took charge of hers.

Carrie closed her eyes, abandoning herself to the magnificent sensations. She met his tongue eagerly as his mouth gave everything and took everything in return, probing, plundering, possessing.

When he released her, Carrie was breathless for the second time that day. She was sure nothing would ever be the same from that moment on.

Jack's eyes looked darker, greener, more intense than Carrie remembered. He glanced toward the front of the boat, adjusted their course slightly, then returned his gaze to Carrie.

"I'm putting you on the first plane out of here," he said.

"What?"

"You heard me. I should have done it the moment there was a hint of trouble. You're in danger, and I won't have it." His words were calm, deliberate, as if the matter were closed and her opinion was of no consequence.

"We're both in danger," Carrie argued. "If I leave, you come with me."

"Now look, Carrie—"

"No, you look. I'm into this thing too deep to back out now. Like it or not, you're stuck with me."

"I shouldn't have involved you—"

"It's too late."

"I want you safe—"

"We'll both be safer if we stick together. How do you know this Claude wouldn't follow me, maybe all the way to Iowa? If he's been keeping an eye on us, he knows I went diving with you today. He has every reason to believe that you showed me something significant regarding the *Laurel*. If he wants that information, a little thing like a trip back to the States isn't going to stop him.

"Besides," she added when she saw that her sensible argument was getting to Jack, "you need me. If I hadn't met Jolly on the beach, if I hadn't thought to ask Dave about a credit-card receipt, you'd still be where you started. You might have gotten a bad tank of air when you were on your own, sixty feet down. Then where would you be?"

Jack sighed and pulled her close again. "All right, I get the message. You don't let anyone push you around, do you?"

"Not any more—ouch!" Carrie looked down in surprise at her toe, which seemed to be in the clutches of a lobster. She shook her foot and flung the beast away. "Where did that come from?"

Jack stifled a chuckle. "That's Myra's lobster. I caught him just before the trouble with you began. I'd forgotten about him. He must have escaped from my bag. Would you mind catching him and putting him in the freezer?"

"Yes, I would mind," Carrie retorted indignantly. "That sucker pinches like a son of a gun."

"Here, then, take the wheel for a minute."

Jack picked up the lobster, which looked every bit as indignant as Carrie felt, and disappeared. He returned a good five minutes later, having pulled on a pair of soft, faded jeans and a polo shirt. He held what looked like a rock in his left hand.

"What's this?" he asked, opening his hand and revealing the piece of coral Carrie had found earlier. "I saw it in your bag when I was straightening up the boat."

"Oh, well, I don't know," Carrie responded, feeling rather silly. "I thought it might be something when I first saw it, but it looks like an ordinary piece of coral now."

"It may look ordinary, but it doesn't feel ordinary." He placed the object in her hand.

"It's heavy!" she exclaimed.

"There's something inside there," Jack said. "Maybe something metal, if we're lucky. How did you know to pick it up?" he asked, looking genuinely puzzled. "You couldn't have told much about the weight underwater."

Carrie shrugged, turning the helm over to Jack. "I don't know. It just looked different, somehow."

Jack just shook his head. "That's amazing. Your first dive, and you instinctively know what to look for better than I do." He slowed the boat as they approached the hotel's private wharf. "You're a treasure hunter's dream, you know that? I'll never go diving without you again."

Carrie smiled at him, idly wishing he meant what he said.

Chapter Five

Jack placed the lobster on Myra's desk with a flourish. She promptly shrieked, then covered her mouth with her hand and let out a muffled oath.

"Jack Harrington, get that thing off my desk."

"Where would you like me to put it?" he asked, smiling amiably. "You did request a lobster, did you not?"

"Yes, but I'd hoped, perhaps foolishly, that it would come packed in ice."

The lobster began to advance across the polished surface of the desk, its antennae wiggling.

Myra stood and backed away from it squeamishly. "Please, Jack, take it to the kitchen."

"If you insist." He shared an amused glance with Carrie, who was herself a safe distance from the lobster, before picking up the creature and handing it to a passing bellman. "Could you put this on ice for Myra, please?"

At the mention of Myra's name, the bellman smiled benevolently. Her name had a way of working magic around the hotel, Jack had noticed, particularly among the male employees.

"Of course," the bellman said, tipping his hat to the ladies before departing.

"Thank you, Jack," Myra said sweetly, now that the lobster was off her desk. She glanced at Carrie for the first time and smirked. "I see you two are still thicker than molasses. You're taking this bodyguard thing seriously, aren't you? Seen any hit men lurking about?"

"As a matter of fact, *we* haven't seen him." Jack placed his hands on the desk and leaned toward Myra. "But *you* have."

Myra's grin faded. "Me? I've seen a hit man? Jack, you've been out in that sun too long."

Jack pulled up a chair for Carrie and one for himself. When they were all seated comfortably, he gave Myra a pointed look. "What do you know about Claude, your French yachtsman?"

Myra shrugged. "He's generous, attentive, very much a gentleman and he's crazy about me. What else do I need to know?"

"For starters, we think he tampered with my scuba tanks. Carrie ran out of air forty feet down this afternoon." Jack's gaze naturally turned to Carrie as his fear for her life came back to him. "I suspect he's also behind the ransacking of Carrie's room."

"And the sabotage of Jack's boat," Carrie added.

Myra's eyes widened, then narrowed. "That isn't possible. What makes you think Claude is responsible?"

"We have our reasons," said Jack. "How much have you told him about us?"

"Well, I never—" Myra started to deny the accusation, then stopped herself. Several seconds of silence followed as she appeared to consider the question. "Claude did express an interest in scuba diving," she said carefully. "and I may have told him a little bit about you..."

"Did you happen to mention we were going to Billy Bones last night?" Jack asked.

"Mmm, it may have come up in conversation. We were sitting in the lobby when you two left last night. I might have made some remark."

"Did you tell him where my boat was being repaired?"

"Y—yes, I did," Myra answered, looking more and more unnerved. "He wanted to know where a good marina was...."

"Could Claude have 'borrowed' your passkey last night?" Carrie asked.

Myra's uncertainty vanished. "No," she said emphatically. "I don't carry that around with me except when I need it, and I keep it locked up at all times, right here." She opened the desk drawer. There was no key in sight. When she looked up, her ebony eyes were wide with a horrified realization. "He took my key. That's how he broke into your room. That stinking crook was just using me to get to you. Well, if he thinks he'll get away with it he's got another thing coming. No one uses Myra Franklin."

She looked at Carrie, her eyes brimming with apology. "I feel so responsible! You weren't hurt, were you?"

Carrie shook her head.

"We know it's not your fault, Myra," Jack said, immediately easing up on the intimidation now that he'd gotten through to her. "But we need your help. What's Claude's last name, and how can we locate him?"

"His last name is Colline," Myra answered. "I don't have a telephone number for him—he hasn't given me one. But I can show you where his yacht is anchored."

She started to get up, but Jack halted her with his hand. "It's too late. He's moved the yacht out of the harbor. Do you remember the name of the boat?"

"I think it's called the *Touché*. He never took me on board."

It turned out that Myra knew precious little about Claude Colline. She was, however, able to provide an accurate physical description: six foot one, heavyset, tanned skin, black hair with graying temples. And jewelry—lots of jewelry.

Carrie nodded as Myra described their adversary. "That's the guy I met at Billy Bones."

"There's one piece of jewelry in particular that's rather distinctive," Myra added. "He wears a gold coin around his neck."

"You mean like a Krugerrand?" Jack asked hopefully.

"No, I mean like a gold doubloon."

A long silence followed. "That indicates a definite interest in treasure," Jack murmured, almost to himself. "He must be after something he thinks I've found, but how would he know about it?"

"Know about what?" Myra asked.

Jack mentally kicked himself. He'd almost spilled the beans, and to Myra, of all people. "Um, Myra," he said, skirting the question, "if you run into Claude again, would you get to a phone as discreetly as possible and call me at my house? Then encourage him to stick around until I get there. I'll never get to the bottom of this until I meet the guy face to face."

Myra seemed eager to help any way she could. "Sure, I can do that."

"And Myra, be careful. The man is dangerous. Don't go anywhere alone with him."

"Hmmf, not on a bet. Not after what I've learned to-day."

A couple of hours later, Carrie was zipping across the island, once again on the back of Jack's red scooter. Though she'd wanted nothing more than to take a hot shower and wash the salt water out of her hair, Jack had convinced her to postpone bathing, and instead to pack a few things and go with him to his small house on the other side of town.

"You'll be safer there," he'd said. "Don't forget, our friend Claude has a passkey."

Carrie had hesitated. Though Jack was the sexiest, most fascinating man she'd ever met and she had looked forward to getting to know him better, she hadn't figured on moving in with him.

"I have a nice guest room all made up," he'd added, as if guessing her thoughts. "We'll go to the waterfront and get some fat shrimp and some vegetables and make shish kebabs. Now you can't turn down an offer like that."

It was true, she couldn't. He was just too persuasive, and she too easy to persuade. The argument she'd been formulating was over before it had started.

So here she was, riding on the back of a scooter with her arms around Jack like some motorcycle mama. Her hair had long since lost its rubber band and was flying out from under the crash helmet in wild disarray. She was sunburned and exhausted and enjoying herself thoroughly.

What would good ol' Web think of her if he saw her now? He might think he was well rid of her. As she leaned her cheek against Jack's broad back, she didn't bother to suppress her mischievous smile.

They browsed at a roadside stand near the waterfront for shrimp and scallops, plump cherry tomatoes, pearl onions and some kind of exotic-looking squash. It was only when they were climbing on board the scooter once again that Carrie saw the police station across the street.

"Jack!" she exclaimed in a sudden burst of inspiration. "Why don't we just go to the police, now that we know Claude Colline's name?"

A pained expression crossed Jack's face as he shook his head. "They won't do anything besides ask a lot of questions about matters I'd rather not discuss just yet."

"But Jack," Carrie persisted, "that man ought to be behind bars. He's dangerous."

"I'm telling you, it won't help to involve the police. We *think* Claude Colline is responsible for sabotage and vandalism, but we don't have proof. Besides, the police don't want to cause trouble for someone as rich and powerful as this Claude appears to be, and they certainly don't want to cause trouble for a foreigner, not based on the puny evidence we have."

"Our evidence isn't puny," Carrie argued. "After all, he did impersonate a government official when I met him."

"You met him in a dark hallway. He didn't give his name. How do you know it was Claude Colline, a man you've never even seen otherwise?"

"Don't tell me *you* don't think it was him!"

Jack placed a soothing arm around her shoulders. "*I* know it was the same man. I'm just trying to show you what the police can do when they start asking questions."

"Well, I don't care. I'd feel so much better if we filed a report or a complaint against Mr. Colline. Maybe the police already have something on him. Anyway, I don't like the idea of you confronting this guy all alone."

Jack gave a defeated sigh. "Okay, you win. But don't say I didn't warn you."

Carrie had good reason to remember Jack's warning a few minutes later, as she attempted to tell a coherent story to the skeptical desk sergeant on duty.

"But Ms. Bishop," the sergeant protested, "if you've only been here a couple of days, why would anyone be trying to harm you?"

"It's not me they want to intimidate, it's Jack."

"And you, Mr. Harrington," the sergeant said, turning his attention toward Jack. "Why would anyone want to cause trouble for you? Do you know this, uh, Claude Colline?"

"No. And I have no idea why he's bothering me. But he most definitely is."

"If you will excuse me a moment," the sergeant said. "Perhaps you will want to speak with Detective Van Horn."

Jack groaned, folded his arms on the desk and leaned his head against them in a gesture of despair.

"What's wrong?" Carrie asked when they were alone. "A detective sounds like just what we need."

Jack remained silent.

The sergeant returned a few minutes later accompanied by a short, round man in a too-tight suit. The newcomer smiled toothily at Carrie and extended his hand. "I'm Detective Clive Van Horn," he said condescendingly. "How can I be of—" Abruptly his voice changed its tone. "Jack Harrington. I might have known you'd be involved in a screwy story like this. All right. Let's go to my office and see if you can turn this convoluted mess into a legitimate complaint."

Jack shook his head. "It's all there in the statement we gave to the sergeant. We don't really expect you to do anything except note the complaint, in case we have any more trouble with this Frenchman—which we most assuredly will. Come on, Carrie, let's get out of here."

Carrie didn't feel inclined to argue. She sensed a definite aura of animosity in the room, and she knew it wouldn't serve their interests to remain and belabor their point. Wordlessly she followed Jack to the scooter, parked in the shade of a palm tree.

"What was that all about?" she finally asked as they secured their groceries to the scooter. "How do you and Van Horn know each other?"

"I was hoping you wouldn't ask that."

"I'm asking. I'm burning with curiosity."

"Well, it was a small matter, really. I was cruising close to shore and my boat ran out of gas at an inopportune moment—I was late getting to the hotel for a scuba class. And here was this other boat tied up to a private dock, with a full five-gallon can of gas just sitting in it, and I sort of borrowed some of the gas."

"Jack! You really are a pirate."

"I fully intended to pay for the gas. In fact, I had a five-dollar bill in my pocket, which I would have left under the gas can if given half a chance. But how was I to know that boat belonged to a police detective? It wasn't a pretty sight when he barreled out of the boat house and caught me."

"No, I imagine not."

Conversation ceased for a time as they continued their journey. Jack guided the scooter away from town and up a steep, winding road dotted with modest stucco houses. The higher they went, the more magnificent the view became. After a few more minutes, Jack pulled into the driveway of a small yellow bungalow-type house and cut the engine.

"So this is your home," Carrie said, admiring the neatly painted house and profusion of color in the flower beds. Most especially she liked the bay window that looked out over the harbor. "Until you told me you had a house, I just assumed you lived on your boat."

"You might say I have two homes," Jack explained, retrieving Carrie's things from the compartment under the scooter's seat. "The house doesn't really belong to me; the university owns it. I lease it for a reasonable sum."

"You must love coming home to this view," Carrie said as she entered the living room and gazed out the bay window. The sun was just beginning to set, casting an orange glow onto the harbor waters and the bobbing boats.

"You know something?" Jack said as he came up behind Carrie and slipped his arms around her waist. "I've never really stopped to admire this view. It's breathtaking."

Carrie felt her heart beating faster at Jack's nearness. She leaned her head against his shoulder and allowed herself to enjoy the moment. It would pass shortly, she knew, and she might never again know the joy of sharing a sunset with Jack Harrington. The thought filled her with an intense, poignant sadness.

"If I had a view like this," she said dreamily, "I'd admire it every day. I'd put aside a few minutes each evening just to sit and watch."

"Mmm. You're making me see how much I take for granted. I've been so wrapped up in my work the past few years that sometimes I don't see what's right in front of my nose."

Carrie turned to face him, finding herself in his embrace. "Right now I'm right in front of your nose." She brought her arms tentatively to his shoulders. "You're not taking me for granted."

"Not a chance of that," he said just before capturing her lips with his.

This kissing stuff was getting to be a habit, Carrie thought dazedly. Her hands moved instinctively to the back of his neck, and her fingers tangled themselves in his springy black hair. She'd deliberately invited this kiss, and now she questioned her own judgment as her body became more involved in the dancing sensations Jack provoked in her.

He moved his lips from her mouth to her neck, exploring the soft flesh below her ear. His mustache tickled in a delightful way, and a small, sensual moan escaped from Carrie's throat. She was stunned at the sound of her own pleasure.

Carrie wasn't sure just when he had reached under her blouse, but she was now aware of his warm, sure fingers touching her breasts through her swimsuit. She trembled uncontrollably with the passion that was swiftly building inside her.

"Do you have any idea what you're doing to me, Carrie Bishop?" Jack's voice was a hoarse whisper.

Carrie had a pretty good idea, and she began to feel the first prickles of apprehension. What had she started? And did she have the control it would take to slow things down, if she wanted to?

The decision was taken out of her hands when Jack gently extricated himself from her entwining arms. "I believe you said something earlier about wanting a bath?" The question was deceptively casual, delivered between his rapid breaths.

"You—were you wanting to join me?" she croaked.

Jack laughed outright. "You are priceless, you know that? As inviting as that proposition sounds, no, that is not what I had in mind. I thought perhaps we could both use a few moments to ourselves."

Carrie had to agree, and she was grateful to Jack for having the sense to read the situation so clearly. She felt as if she was dangling a brightly burning match over a tank of gasoline—gasoline she hadn't known existed until yesterday.

"The bath is that way," he said, pointing toward a hall-way. "The bedroom to the right is yours. There should be plenty of towels and soap. I'll get the charcoal started."

He watched her walk away from him with a mixture of relief and regret. When he'd asked Carrie to dinner that first day, he had viewed it as a pleasant diversion. A few hours in her company, however, had disabused him of that notion. "Pleasant" was much too mild a word to describe Carrie. She was captivating. Bewitching. Addictive.

She was like a narcotic to his system, so that the more he saw of her, the more he listened to her soft voice and watched the lights dancing in her mischievous eyes, the more he needed her. She made him feel emotions that ran deep.

Those strange feelings were taking him into uncharted territory, and he thought of it like diving into an unexplored underwater cave—exhilarating and slightly frightening. The experiences he shared with Carrie had led to a unique sort of bonding that was alien to Jack's nature and yet intriguing nonetheless.

Even his physical desire for her was unique. Wanting a woman was nothing new to him, yet surely the fierceness of his desire for Carrie was like nothing he'd ever experienced. All day he had ached to see and touch all those maddeningly secret places she kept covered with that prim white swimsuit.

Carrie was a giving, loving soul, and he was sure she found him desirable as well. If he merely asked, she might willingly make love to him with all the innate sweetness and passion that were in her. He'd been tempted, just now, to test that theory, but something had held him back. That's why he'd put on the brakes—to allow Carrie as well as him-self more time to consider just exactly what they were doing.

Even though Carrie would be leaving the island in a week, this newfound alliance was not and never would be a sim-

ple fling, regardless of whether they shared a sexual relationship. Two people could walk away from a fling
unscathed. It was too late for that with him and Carrie. In
some indefinable way, she had already begun to change him,
to bind him to her with thousands of tiny silken threads.

The question was, did he want to be changed? Did he
want to feel bound by all these feelings roiling around inside him, or would it be better if the sensitive side of him
remained buried? It had been years since he'd felt responsible to anyone or anything besides himself. Now he was responsible for Carrie's safety, and he wasn't exactly
comfortable with that role.

Jack made a pile of charcoal briquettes in his hibachi,
soaked them with starter fluid and threw a match on top. He
stared into the resulting flames, trying to make sense of the
confusion. But after several minutes of contemplation, he
was no closer to an answer than when he'd begun.

He did know one thing, he concluded as he began to peel
and devein the shrimp. For the first time in years he was
feeling passionate about something besides his underwater
endeavors. Maybe that was good for him. Then again . . .

Carrie appeared a short time later in a pair of soft, faded
jeans and an oversized red T-shirt, one of her island souvenirs. Her hair was wrapped in a towel. "I'm going pretty
casual tonight," she said, shrugging apologetically. "Hope
you don't mind."

Jack wasn't thinking of her clothes so much as what was
under her clothes. She had brought a clean, soapy smell into
the kitchen with her. When she unwrapped her wet hair
from the towel, the intriguing scent of her green-apple
shampoo permeated the room.

"I made up a batch of frozen margaritas," Jack said, resisting the urge to go to her, touch her. "They're in the

blender, so help yourself. I think I'll jump in the shower myself.''

Carrie threw her towel over her shoulder and poured herself a margarita in the salted glass Jack had prepared, then wandered out to the patio in back, where the coals smoked invitingly in the hibachi. She sat in a wooden deck chair and combed out her hair, allowing the mild trade breeze to dry it into its naturally unruly waves.

The time she'd spent standing under the pounding hot shower had thankfully given her a little perspective. Just because she was under Jack's roof, that didn't mean she should share his bed. Though the idea was inviting, she had to consider the impact a physical act of love would have on her, on Jack and on the relationship itself.

She and Jack had grown unexpectedly close in the past couple of days. She found him exciting, intelligent, virile—definitely virile—but kind and compassionate, too. In short, he was the kind of man with whom she could easily form permanent bonds.

And that was the problem. Their relationship was by definition temporary.

Carrie's teeth worried her lower lip as she tried to analyze the dilemma from every direction. The wisest, most prudent course of action was to keep herself and Jack a safe distance apart. The prospect was unappealing at best.

''Hey, why the frown?''

Carrie looked up suddenly to find Jack standing before her. He had an uncanny knack for materializing as if right out of her dreams, though he looked more appetizing than a figment of her imagination could. He smelled good, too, like lime shaving cream. She felt her resolve wavering.

''I was thinking about us,'' she said truthfully.

''With that frown? That doesn't bode well.''

ACCEPT FOUR BRAND NEW
YOURS

We'd like to send you four free Silhouette novels, worth $9.00, to introduce you to the benefits of the Silhouette Reader Service.™ We hope your free books will convince you to subscribe, but that's up to you. Accepting them places you under no obligation to buy anything, but we hope you'll want to continue your membership in the Reader Service.

So unless we hear from you, once a month we'll send you six additional Silhouette Romance™ novels to read and enjoy. If you choose to keep them, you'll pay just $2.25* per volume. And there is *no* charge for shipping and handling. There are *no* hidden extras! You may cancel at any time, for any reason, just by sending us a note or a shipping statement marked "cancel" or by returning any shipment of books to us at our cost. Either way the free books and gifts are yours to keep!

ALSO FREE!
ACRYLIC DIGITAL CLOCK/CALENDAR

As a free gift simply to thank you for accepting four free books we'll send you this stylish digital quartz clock — a handsome addition to any decor!

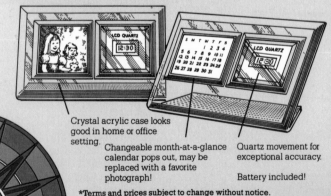

Crystal acrylic case looks good in home or office setting.

Changeable month-at-a-glance calendar pops out, may be replaced with a favorite photograph!

Quartz movement for exceptional accuracy.

Battery included!

*Terms and prices subject to change without notice.

Sales taxes applicable in NY and Iowa.

© 1990 HARLEQUIN ENTERPRISES LIM

SILHOUETTE ROMANCE™ NOVELS
FREE!

 Silhouette Reader Service™

```
AFFIX
FOUR FREE BOOKS
STICKER HERE
```

YES, send me my four free books and gifts as explained on the opposite page. I have affixed my "free books" sticker above and my two "free gift" stickers below. I understand that accepting these books and gifts places me under no obligation ever to buy any books; I may cancel at any time, for any reason, and the free books and gifts will be mine to keep!

215 CIS HAYG (U-S-R-01/90)

NAME
                                    (PLEASE PRINT)

ADDRESS   APT.

CITY

STATE   ZIP

Offer limited to one per household and not valid to current Silhouette Romance™ subscribers. All orders subject to approval.

```
AFFIX FREE
CLOCK/CALENDAR
STICKER HERE
```

```
AFFIX FREE
MYSTERY GIFT
STICKER HERE
```

PRINTED IN U.S.A.

WE EVEN PROVIDE FREE POSTAGE!

It costs you *nothing* to send for your free books — we've paid the postage on the attached reply card. And we'll pick up the postage on your shipment of free books and gifts, and also on any subsequent shipments of books, should you choose to become a subscriber. Unlike many book clubs, we charge *nothing* for postage and handling!

She smiled. "Maybe I was frowning because the smoke from the fire was getting in my eyes. Come on, let's get those shish kebabs on the road. I think the coals are about ready."

Dinner was a surprisingly relaxed affair, given its prelude, Carrie thought. She cooked up a pot of rice while Jack threaded the shrimp and vegetables onto wooden skewers. When the kebabs were lined up on the grill and basted with teriyaki sauce, Jack and Carrie reclined in deck chairs and waited patiently for dinner. They spoke pleasantly as darkness descended on the patio, but Carrie's doubts about herself and Jack and their precarious situation were never far from her mind.

The shish kebabs turned out to be delicious. "This is ambrosia," Carrie said, popping another shrimp into her mouth.

"Here, have another kebab," Jack offered.

She held up her hand. "No, please. I'm stuffed as it is."

"An after-dinner drink, then," Jack suggested, standing and taking Carrie's plate. "I have some banana liqueur that'll knock your socks off."

"But I'm not wearing socks," she said, wiggling her bare toes playfully.

"Maybe it'll knock something else off, then." His suggestive tone gave her pause for a moment until he winked. "Or maybe you'd prefer coffee."

In the end they both opted for the liqueur, which Carrie found quite palatable, and retired to the living room. Jack spread several large throw pillows onto the rug in front of the bay window, and they reclined side by side to gaze out at the sparkling harbor.

"Now that you've pointed out this view to me, I think I'm addicted," Jack said.

"I don't understand how you could take this for granted," said Carrie, marveling at the thousands of jewels of light twinkling in and around the midnight-blue harbor.

"You have to understand, Carrie, that I had other things on my mind when I came here. Before I made contact with the University of the Virgin Islands, I'd been wandering aimlessly all over the Caribbean. I knew I wanted to make some great discovery, but I was so busy trying to scratch out a living, teaching diving classes and doing small salvage operations, that I didn't have time to do the exploring I wanted.

"When the university offered to *pay* me to explore and map shipwrecks around the islands, I could hardly believe my luck. I've been going at it with a vengeance."

"And now you think you're close to finding something important?"

He shrugged. "The *Laurel* is the most interesting thing I've found in six years."

"It's fine to have a goal," she said carefully, "but such single-minded determination can't possibly be good for you."

"I know that." He slipped his arm around her shoulders and drew her closer to him. "Especially now I know that. You've made me see how much I'm missing."

They were silent for a time, each lost in thought, until Carrie spoke again. "Jack, if we'd met somewhere else—in Des Moines, for instance—under more ordinary circumstances, do you think we'd be spending time together?"

Jack thought for a moment. "I can't speak for you," he answered, "but I know how I'd feel. I'd still want to be with you."

Carrie liked that answer. She relaxed a little. After a few more moments of silence, she asked another question, one that had been on her mind all evening. "Have you thought about us making love?"

Jack's eyebrows rose in surprised arches. "In all honesty, I've thought about it on and off since the moment we met, and I've thought of little else this evening."

"Then I'm not imagining things—there is a special spark of something between us. What I'm trying to figure out is what's holding us in check. Something is. I feel it."

Jack took a steadying sip of his liqueur. The woman certainly had cut right to the heart of the matter. "I don't know quite what to make of your honesty, Carrie. I'm not accustomed to dealing with such straightforwardness."

"If you'd rather I just shut up—"

"No, please, I'd like you to keep talking. You seem to be onto something."

Carrie opened her mouth to continue her line of thought, then closed it again. Everything had seemed clear in her mind a moment before, but now her thoughts were muddled again. Still, she made a stab at it. "In the short time I've known you, I've come to feel very... attached, perhaps unreasonably so. I'm already sad at the thought of leaving the islands, and you. If we made love it would draw us closer. I'm afraid to get any closer, because the eventual goodbye would be that much more difficult. Does that make sense?"

Jack sighed. "Unfortunately, it makes perfect sense." He knew it was his turn to voice his thoughts. He owed Carrie honesty. But honest, personal dialogue wasn't something he was accustomed to. He hadn't talked about his feelings to anyone in years.

His words came haltingly, and Carrie could tell that he was making a great effort for her benefit.

"Without even trying," he said, "you've drawn me partway out of a shell that I've been hiding in for a long time.

You mentioned closeness. We *are* close, Carrie, and I have mixed feelings about it. I enjoy being with you, but I'm not sure I'm ready to be close to anyone. I have too many things to work out first.''

Carrie's reaction was to reach for Jack's hand and squeeze it.

"Don't get me wrong," he continued. "I'm glad we met. But you scare the hell out of me. So despite the fact that I want you—make no mistake about that—I know it's better not to rush anything."

To his relief, Carrie smiled. "Hmmf. You, the big bad adventurer, Jack Harrington, scared by me?"

He couldn't resist. He had to kiss her. But even as he gently explored her soft, inviting lips, another part of him kept a tight rein on his rampant desires.

"There is something else I want to know about you, Carrie," he said a few minutes later. "Why did you come on this vacation alone?"

Carrie thought about that for a moment. "Maybe I *was* looking for a little excitement," she admitted. "But mostly I planned this trip to prove to myself that I could live life to the fullest—without a man. I'm not doing a very good job, am I?"

"I'm not so sure. You probably would have been much better off if you'd signed up for tennis lessons instead of scuba diving. Then you never would have laid eyes on me and you wouldn't be involved in this mess."

Carrie leaned on one elbow and looked him in the eye. "I wouldn't trade this mess for anything in the world."

Chapter Six

Jack awoke with a start. Where was he? Sunlight flooded the room in which he found himself, and a cuddly female form was nestled against his chest. It took him only a few moments to remember that he and Carrie had lain by the bay window until the wee hours, alternately talking, kissing and finally, apparently, sleeping.

He smiled at the memory, but the smile lasted only until he consulted his watch. It was eight-thirty.

He looked at Carrie, sleeping peacefully against him. She appeared as trouble-free and innocent as a child, which made it doubly hard to wake her. He would have liked to kiss her awake, slowly, and to share a leisurely breakfast with her. But time wasn't on his side this morning.

"Carrie?"

Definitely still asleep, she snuggled closer.

"Carrie, sweetheart. Wake up." He shook her gently, then a little harder.

"Hmm? Oh, good morning. Morning! What time is it?" She sat up groggily and rubbed her eyes, then glanced at her watch. "Oh, dear." She looked up hopefully. "Is the coffee ready?"

Jack couldn't help smiling. She looked undeniably appealing this morning. The sun shone on her hair, transforming it into an unruly golden cloud around her face. Sleep had shifted her souvenir T-shirt slightly askew, revealing a hint of her sun-kissed shoulder.

"Unfortunately we don't have time for coffee, sleepyhead. I have a scuba class in less than an hour, and Myra does not tolerate tardiness." He pulled a reluctant Carrie to her feet, then drew her close. She went limp as a rag doll in his arms, closing her eyes and sighing contentedly against his shoulder.

"Not a fast waker-upper, are you?" he murmured. What would it be like, he wondered, to awaken with this woman in his bed, to make love to her and watch as desire slowly brought her body into awareness? His blood surged, and he had to force himself not to pick her up and carry her into the bedroom.

Before he could change his mind, he grasped her by the shoulders and stood her upright. "Much as I'd like to dawdle with you, we've got to get going."

Carrie came more fully awake, savoring the way Jack's presence enveloped her like a soft quilt, amazed at how comfortable she was with him. She'd never felt this relaxed around her husband, even after years of marriage! The sheer rightness of waking up with Jack was enough to bowl her over.

She felt a twinge of disappointment, too. She had hoped for a slower, more intimate morning—especially given the things they'd shared last night. True, they hadn't made love, but they'd talked until all hours and she'd told him things about herself she hadn't confided to anyone, things about her ill-fated marriage and her own self-doubts. In turn, he had talked about the joy he once found in hunting for sunken treasure, and she felt she was beginning to understand how joy had turned to bitterness when he'd lost his Florida galleon to Charlie Hill.

She would have liked to learn more, but she recognized the note of urgency in Jack's manner and knew this wasn't a time for quiet conversation. She forced herself to get in gear, splashing water on her face and sliding her feet into sandals. She grabbed her things and they were off.

Jack made up for lost time by taking back roads and pushing the scooter at full throttle. At every corner goats and chickens cleared a path for them. By the time they reached the hotel, Carrie was more wide awake than if she'd drunk an entire pot of caffeine-laden coffee.

"You can let go now. We've stopped," Jack said after pulling into a parking place.

Relieved, Carrie loosened her crushing grip on Jack's rib cage. "It's nice that you're so conscientious about punctuality on the job, but you could have at least slowed down for the chickens."

"They got out of the way," he replied calmly, stowing the crash helmets under the seat.

Carrie shuddered, remembering how the sea of white feathers had miraculously parted just in time. At least she and Jack were still in one piece.

Jack led the way toward the hotel's private boat house, and for the first time Carrie wondered what she wanted to do that day. Part of her wanted to remain with Jack wherever he went, but another, more sensible part told her she was pushing when she shouldn't.

"You'll be an old pro when we go diving today," Jack commented as they descended a flight of stairs that led toward the dock.

"You expect me to get near a scuba tank after what happened yesterday?"

He paused at the bottom of the stairs and took her hand. "I know you had quite a scare, but things like that don't happen every day. You'll be safe. Dave said he'd keep my tanks under lock and key. No one could tamper with them."

Carrie hesitated. Jack did make her feel safe, standing here on the walkway. But in open water? "I don't think I can go underwater again. I'm too scared."

"It's just like falling off a horse," he argued. "You have to get right back on or—"

"Tomorrow," she said decisively, buying herself a little more time to work up her courage. "I promise I'll dive tomorrow."

Jack started to voice more objections, then relented as they resumed walking. "I'll hold you to that. Tell you what. Today you can drive the boat and help me with the equipment."

"No, Jack. I'd really prefer to keep my feet on dry land today. I'd like to do some sight-seeing. After all, this is a vacation."

Jack stopped again and turned abruptly, looking just the slightest bit put out. "I want you with me, where I can keep an eye out for you."

"I'll be careful."

"That's not good enough."

"I'll hire a taxi for the day," she said, inspired. "I won't go anywhere alone."

Jack seemed to consider this for a moment. The tense lines of his face softened. "If you're intent on this sight-seeing business, at least do me this favor. Ask Myra to get in touch with my friend Gifford. He's the old man I told you about yesterday, the diver who knows about the *Laurel*. He drives a taxi now. I trust him to take care of you."

As much as Carrie bristled at Jack's proprietary attitude, she was warmed by his concern. "All right," she agreed. "That sounds fair. And you'll be careful, too?" He nodded.

Impulsively Carrie stood on tiptoe to peck him on the cheek, then turned quickly away before she could change her mind. She felt Jack's eyes on her, watching to see that she was safe as she retraced her steps to the hotel. She found herself wishing she hadn't been so obstinate just now. It wouldn't have been so bad, driving the boat.

But tying herself to Jack when it wasn't absolutely necessary would have been just plain foolish. She'd already admitted that she was feeling unreasonably close to him, and after the wonderful, intimate things they'd shared last night, she felt more connected to him than ever. She was setting herself up for a terrible fall when the time came for them to say goodbye. The only antidote that came to mind was to put distance between them.

"You're Gifford?" Carrie asked the tall, grizzled black man who emerged from the green taxi. Her first thought was that he looked like a telephone pole with clothes. He had to be six foot six if he was an inch, and his neat khaki pants and shirt appeared so loose she wondered why they didn't fall off.

His calm brown eyes continued to study her for a moment, just as hers did him. "Yes, I am Gifford," he finally answered with a lilting calypso accent. "And you must be Miss Bishop. I believe I am to take you sight-seeing this morning?"

Carrie nodded, allowing him to gallantly open her door and tuck her safely inside.

"So I hear you've had some excitement on your vacation," he said as he climbed into the car.

"You could call it that," she replied dryly, wondering how much Jack had told this man and how he'd managed it.

"Well, we won't talk about such unpleasantness this morning." He pulled out onto the road. "I'm here to entertain and enlighten. Where shall I take you?"

Carrie had no clear idea of what she wanted to see, so Gifford took her on a meandering drive in and around the hills of St. Thomas. She found herself relaxing under the spell of Gifford's colorful narration of island history and folklore as she took dozens of snapshots of the fascinating people and places.

When it was lunchtime they wound up in downtown Charlotte Amalie. Carrie insisted they park the cab and walk through the bustling streets to one of the outdoor cafés she'd seen. "I'll buy," she offered the reluctant Gifford. "And you can tell me more about yourself. Have you lived here all your life?"

"Yes, miss, all seventy-three years." He left the cab unlocked and followed her lead.

"How long have you known Jack?" she asked as they strolled unhurriedly along the sidewalk. Carrie struggled to make her tone light, though learning more about Jack had somehow become a priority in her life, as if knowing more concrete facts about him would somehow help her explain away the vivid attraction she felt for him.

"It seems I've known Jack all my life," Gifford responded thoughtfully. "Perhaps that is because in him I see a bit of myself when I was younger. Believe it or not, I was something of a renegade in my day." He smiled sheepishly at Carrie, and she returned the smile, genuinely liking this man with his courtly manners. "But in actual time, I suppose I've known him a little over a year, since he showed up on St. Thomas without a dime in his pocket and a burning desire to instantly know everything there was to know about the Virgin Islands. He is not such a patient man."

Carrie picked a café at random—they all looked inviting—and Gifford held her chair for her at a small metal table in the shade of a palm tree.

"Oh, I don't know, he can be patient," Carrie responded, remembering his tenderness from last night. He hadn't pushed her toward the bedroom, though she knew he'd wanted her. The desire had zinged between them like an electric current.

Gifford's unexpected laughter was so loud and rich it made the metal table vibrate. Carrie had the uncomfortable sensation that he'd somehow known the very private thoughts she'd just formulated, and she felt herself flushing slightly.

To disguise her discomfiture she made a grab for the tattered menu stuck between the salt and pepper shakers.

"Not meaning to be nosy, Miss," Gifford said cautiously as he perused his own menu, "but how long have *you* known Jack?"

"Only a couple of days." *And one very nice night,* she added silently.

"He's a good man, Jack. Do you have, ah, some sort of business with him?"

That question again. Carrie's prickles of apprehension returned with a vengeance. "Why does everyone ask me that?" she said, careful to keep her tone curious rather than irritated. "Jack's been nice enough to show me around a little—that's all. Suddenly everyone I meet wants to know what my business is with him!"

Gifford's amusement was evident. "Perhaps it is be
cause we are not used to seeing Jack with a companion
particularly a woman. He is a bit of a loner. I meant noth
ing disrespectful by the question, Miss. It was merely an ol
man's curiosity."

Carrie relaxed some, warmed by the knowledge that Jacl
wasn't in the habit of squiring around female tourists.

The spicy chowder and crisp conch fritters Gifford rec
ommended for lunch were marvelous. Carrie committed the
tastes and textures to her memory—something else for he
mental scrapbook—then pushed her plate away and sighe
contentedly. While Gifford nursed his beer and gazed pen
sively at the passersby, Carrie absently leafed through
discarded local newspaper she'd found on the next table.

A line of bold type in the want ads caught her eye
"LIBRARIAN. Part-time. Some experience preferred. Ap
ply in person, University of the Virgin Islands Library."

Suddenly the door to a world of possibilities opened u
in Carrie's mind. Could an ordinary person like herself ac
tually secure a job and make a living on a Caribbean island'

She was qualified for that job; she'd worked part-time fo
three years in the library at the community college she'd at
tended after marrying Web, to complete her impractica
history degree. Upon her graduation, Web had convince
her to quit the library and do volunteer work at the hospita
gift shop, which he considered more appropriate for he
position as his wife. The gift shop was all right, and she'
even proved herself so competent that she'd been promote
to a paying managerial position—much to Web's chagrin
But she'd missed the library, she realized. How wonderfu
to once again be close to the history books she loved.

"Are you ready to go, Miss?" Gifford's words intrude
on Carrie's intriguing line of thought.

She closed the newspaper. "Ready if you are. How about showing me the university this afternoon?" she asked on impulse.

"Certainly, I can do that. But are you sure you wouldn't prefer Coral World? I thought you were rather committed to the idea earlier."

"I'll see that another day," she answered airily. "Anyway, the sky is clouding up. I think we're in for some rain."

The university's one-hundred-seventy-five-acre campus was larger and more modern than Carrie had expected. Gifford parked the taxi at her request, but declined to wander the campus with her.

"I will remain here, if you don't mind," he said. "I am afraid my old bones aren't up to all this walking."

"All right," Carrie agreed. "I won't take long."

She didn't really intend to enter the library, but when she stumbled across it the temptation was just too strong. Neither did she intend to speak to anyone about the job, but as she stood just inside the entrance, inhaling the pleasant, distinctive odor of books, a kind-faced older woman smiled warmly at her from the circulation desk.

"Can I help you find something?" the woman asked in appropriately hushed tones.

Carrie approached the desk and introduced herself. "I saw the advertisement for the part-time librarian..." She let her voice trail off when she saw the puzzled look on the woman's face. "Oh, I'm not here to apply for the job," Carrie added hastily as she realized that her Hawaiian shorts, bright yellow blouse and sandals were hardly appropriate for a job interview. "At least, not exactly. I'm only here on vacation. But..."

The librarian gave her a knowing smile. "But the thought has occurred that you wouldn't mind living here."

"Yes, that's exactly right," Carrie said, realizing how preposterous the whole idea was. "It's probably just a fantasy. But I thought it wouldn't hurt to at least look into employment possibilities. I worked at a college library for three years," she added.

The librarian smiled warmly. "I'd be happy to tell you about the job. First let me show you around. By the way, I'm Grace Calhoun," she offered as she lead the way toward the stacks. Several students sat hunched around tables, studying with an intensity that could only mean it was exam time.

"If it'll make you feel any less crazy," Grace continued, "I was in your shoes ten years ago. My husband and I came here on a cruise, and six months later we chucked our jobs and moved here for good. We haven't regretted the decision, either."

So it was possible, Carrie mused. "Just out of curiosity, would I be able to make a living as a part-time librarian?" she asked boldly, taking in the haphazard shelving arrangements and untidy rows of books. She could have so much fun putting things in order.

"It depends on how you define a living," Grace answered. "I'll be honest and tell you the money's not terrific. But you can always take in typing or assist some professors in their research to make a little extra. You could survive."

Carrie let this soak in as she surveyed the microfilm library and the new computer system. She asked Grace several questions related to circulation control, acquisition policies and the organization of historical references.

"If you're interested in history books, I'll have to show you one other thing. Come with me." She led the way to a locked room in the back, which contained some of the older, rare books. She opened the door and allowed Carrie a glance inside.

Something about the room intrigued Carrie, drew her through the door. A battered desk sat in back of the room, the top of which was strewn with all manner of papers, open books, index cards and writing utensils.

"Is that your desk?" Carrie asked, drawing closer to the cluttered piece of furniture.

Grace laughed. "Not hardly. That belongs to Professor Harrington. And if you value your life you won't touch it. His work is sacrosanct around here—"

Carrie whirled around. "Did you say Professor Harrington?" Surely not. The idea was ludicrous.

"Why, yes. Jack Harrington. The title of professor is strictly honorary, because he doesn't teach any classes. He just does a lot of research for the university—something to do with shipwrecks."

Almost unconsciously, Carrie reached a hand toward an old map that was unfurled across the desktop, weighted down by a mason jar full of pencils on one corner and a coffee cup, its contents of questionable age, on another.

"Seriously, Carrie, I wouldn't touch anything," Grace warned. "He's very particular, and he swears there's some kind of order to that chaos."

Carrie drew back her hand guiltily and hastened out of the room. "I'm sorry," she said, glancing over her shoulder for one final peek as Grace closed and locked the door. "It's just that I love old books and things—" Her speech was cut short as she plowed headlong into someone striding around the corner.

"Why, speak of the devil," said Grace, just as Carrie looked up into the familiar green eyes, eyes filled with confusion at the moment.

"Carrie! What on earth are you doing here?" Jack asked as he steadied her.

"Oh, you two know each other." Grace eyed the couple with undisguised curiosity. But then a loud throat-clearing at the circulation desk claimed her attention. "Someone's waiting to check out a book. Excuse me a moment."

"I happen to like libraries," Carrie replied to Jack's question, glossing over the real reason she'd come. She was not yet ready to confess to Jack her foolish notion of moving to St. Thomas. "Why aren't you teaching your afternoon scuba class?"

"Canceled, on account of the storm that's coming." His eyes narrowed suspiciously. "Where's Gifford?"

"Waiting for me in the parking lot. Oh, don't look at me like that. I'm safe. Who would accost me in a library? And what are you doing here, anyway... Professor?" She stifled a giggle.

"I had a hunch about something and came here to check—what's so funny?"

"I didn't know you were a bookworm, that's all. The picture just doesn't jibe with the image of the rough, tough adventurer."

"There are lots of things you don't know about me," he whispered, taking her hand and grazing the knuckles against his lips.

Carrie sobered immediately. There probably were a million things she didn't know about Jack, things she'd never learn in the short time they would have together. How would he make love to her, for instance? Would it be soft and sweet, a leisurely sampling of sensual delights? Or would it be like a powerful thunderstorm that built, broke with furious intensity, then slowed to a gentle rain?

Her wayward thoughts produced a flush of heat in her face. Inwardly scolding herself, she slipped her hand away from Jack's and pushed a strand of blond hair off her forehead. Putting physical distance between them had done nothing to dull the emotional closeness she felt. It was a lost cause.

"I have to get back to Gifford," she said, taking a deep breath to clear her mind. "He's been sitting alone in that parking lot an awfully long time. He must be bored to tears." She started for the door, with Jack right behind her. "Then you can tell me about the hunch you wanted to check on. Maybe I can help you."

Grace waved at them as they headed outside, calling softly, "Let me hear from you, Carrie."

Jack raised an eyebrow at that, but said nothing. Determinedly, he recaptured her hand.

The rain hadn't started yet, but the sky was heavy with a blanket of leaden clouds. From a distance Carrie could see that she'd worried about Gifford for nothing. He'd found someone to talk to, a tall, thin boy on a bicycle.

"Gifford always manages to amuse himself," Jack commented as they neared the taxi. "There's always some kid hanging around, eager to hear one of his stories."

But Carrie scarcely heard Jack's words. Her eyes were fixed on the boy, whose posture and mannerisms had taken on a certain element of familiarity. A split second later she recognized him and, pulling her hand away from Jack's once again, she broke into a run.

"Carrie, what the—" Jack called after her, but she didn't slow down or turn. All of her attention was focused on reaching the boy before he got away from her again. But he saw her coming and abruptly took flight long before she was close enough to stop him.

Carrie ran only a few strides before she saw that chasing him was hopeless. She was much too slow on foot, and the bicycle could easily outmaneuver a car. Defeated, she turned toward the taxi, where Jack and Gifford stood side by side, staring at her as if she were crazy.

"Do you know that boy?" she asked Gifford. "Do you know his name?"

Gifford shrugged and answered in the casual, unhurried island manner that at this moment irritated Carrie no end. "I know him slightly. I often tell stories to the local children, stories about the old days of sailing ships and pirates. Roger is one of my more dedicated fans. I do not know his last name."

"That was Jolly, the saboteur," she explained to both men, who nodded, finally understanding her peculiar behavior. "Gifford, what were you and Roger talking about just now?"

"It was nothing of note. The boy was asking me about a shipwreck he'd heard of, off St. John."

Carrie and Jack groaned simultaneously. "What did you tell him?" Jack asked.

Gifford chuckled. "I didn't have much of a chance to tell him anything. The young lady chased him off too quickly."

"Thank goodness for that." Jack put his arm around the old man's thin shoulders as the first fat raindrops began to fall. "Gifford, there's something about that shipwreck..." He paused and looked at Carrie, as if unsure whether to continue.

Carrie knew Jack found it difficult to confide in anyone, even Gifford, whom he claimed to trust. But if Gifford was as knowledgeable about the waters around here as Jack had said, he might be in a position to help solve the mystery. She gave a nod of encouragement to Jack.

Jack took a deep breath, then briefly explained the recent incidents related to the *Laurel*.

Gifford looked perplexed at first, but as Jack concluded his story, the lines of the old man's face fell into a satisfied smile, as if the pieces of a puzzle had just fit themselves together in his mind. "So that is what you're up to."

"I should have told you about it sooner, Gif," Jack said uneasily. "But you know how closed-mouthed I can be."

"There's nothing wrong with keeping some things to yourself," Gifford said, smiling as if he knew a secret or two himself. "Now, we're getting wet. Am I dismissed?"

Carrie reached into her purse and pulled out enough cash to cover the price she and Gifford had agreed upon, plus some extra. She pressed it into his hand. "You're a wonderful tour guide."

"I'm the best. You call me when you are ready to see Coral World."

Jack thanked him, too. Then Gifford folded his tall frame into the taxi and left.

A few minutes later, Jack sat behind his battered desk in a red leather chair, its casters squeaking loudly every time he shifted his weight. He had cleared a spot off the desk only big enough so that he could prop his feet up without getting heel marks on the map. A fat manila folder was open on his lap, apparently forgotten for the moment.

"Sure, now I remember," he said. "When I first came to St. Thomas, a kid named Roger used to constantly beg me to take him diving. I explained to him that he was too young and I couldn't take the responsibility for him, but he wouldn't take no for an answer. I got pretty tough with him, finally, and I haven't seen him since. But he was a little kid, maybe only ten years old—and short."

"Kids grow," Carrie observed. She was perched gingerly on the edge of a not-too-sturdy credenza. "I'll bet you anything it's the same Roger. Do you know his last name?"

Jack sighed. "I never thought to ask him his last name. Island people are generally lax about that formality."

"Then we're back where we started." She slid off the credenza and began to peruse the titles of the cracked volumes in Jack's private cache of books. Outside, the rainstorm raged in earnest. "I used to be a librarian. I bet you didn't know that about me."

"I thought you worked in a gift shop."

"I do now," Carrie said. "But back when I was still in school, and my husband was working sixteen-hour days at the hospital, the library was my refuge. When I wasn't working or studying there, I was poring over history books—the weirder, the more obscure, the better."

"Really?" Jack sounded genuinely surprised and delighted at this new aspect of Carrie's character. "I knew you studied history in college, but I hadn't pegged you for a scholar."

"I'm not a true scholar. More like a dilettante in history." She looked around the room, exhilarated to be inside this storehouse of antique knowledge. The fact that this was Jack's study, infused with his presence, no doubt contributed to her reaction, Carrie mused. "When I first saw this room of yours, my hands itched to touch these dusty old books and maps. And even though Grace Calhoun said you claim to be organized—in your own fashion—I have this tremendous urge to straighten up in here." She turned on him, accusing. "Really, how long has that coffee cup been sitting there growing things?"

"It's been a while since I've had time to devote to the research end of my work," Jack said defensively. "Ever since I found the artifacts at the *Laurel* site, I've been spending every spare moment diving, trying to find some other piece of the puzzle that would explain everything. Speaking of which, I almost forgot."

He reached into the pocket of his windbreaker and pulled out a nondescript black and silver lump. He studied it briefly, then handed it to Carrie. "These are for you. Genuine pieces of eight."

It took her a moment, but finally she recognized the lump for what it was—two stacks of irregularly shaped silver coins, fused together.

"That's what was inside the piece of coral you picked up yesterday," he explained. "I finally had the time today to take the coral to my lab and work on it. I knew there was something inside that lump, but I had no idea it would be this interesting. Look, you can still see some detail."

Carrie held the lump of silver under Jack's desk lamp and peered at the top coins. She could make out the likeness of a ship on each one, and a date, 1749. "That's the same date as on the gold piece you found, isn't it?"

Jack nodded. "When you find a bunch of coins with the same date, it usually indicates a shipment from a Central or South American mint, which would mean the shipwreck occurred shortly after that date. That's the hunch I've been checking on." He thumped the folder in his lap with his finger.

"But the *Laurel* sank a hundred and fifty years too late—" Carrie started to object, then realized what Jack was hinting at. "You mean there might be another shipwreck?"

Jack shrugged. "It was just a hunch. But sometimes hunches don't pan out. If there was another wreck near the *Laurel* site, I can't find even a scrap of evidence. But I wasn't really expecting to. The only time the Spanish flotillas came near these waters was on their way to the New World—before they'd picked up any treasure."

"What about a pirate ship?" Carrie asked, feeling her excitement about the mystery growing.

Jack nodded, acknowledging the remark. "Now that's a thought. It's conceivable a pirate ship full of treasure could have gone to pieces on the reef without anyone knowing. Possible, but not likely."

"Why don't you let me take a crack at it?" Carrie offered casually.

"Pardon?"

"Let me paw through your dusty files. Maybe a fresh eye can come up with a different angle." She turned her back to him and pulled a large, leather-bound volume off a shelf. It's title was *Shipwrecks of the Eighteenth Century*, and it had been published in 1820, according to the copyright.

"You'd waste your vacation holed up in a library?" Jack asked incredulously.

"I would, at least part of the time. Then you'd be free to look for artifacts while I try to make sense of what you find. Anyway, research is never a waste of time, not for me."

"What about us?" Jack asked.

Carrie's skin began to tingle as she heard him quietly stand and come up behind her. He wrapped his arms around her waist and nuzzled her ear. "I'd much rather have you with me than rattling around by yourself in this dusty room."

So much for physical distance, Carrie mused. Calmly she replaced the book on the shelf. She turned slowly, until she was facing him, secure in the tight circle of his arms.

"We'll work it out," she said softly, raising her chin for the kiss she knew was coming. Jack lowered his head, then stopped as his lips were only a breath above hers.

"This offer to do research—it's not a strategy to get you out of scuba diving tomorrow, is it?" he asked with a teasing smile.

"This is an offer of help you sorely need, judging from the condition of this room." She wrinkled her nose. "I plan to go diving tomorrow as I promised, if you still want me. Then you can turn me loose on the research."

Abruptly a black scowl crossed Jack's face. He released Carrie and turned away from her. "I swore once I'd never take on another partner, not under any circumstances, nor for any reason."

"Then don't think of me as a partner," Carrie offered. "I don't want to lay claim to any part of your treasure. Whatever we find is all yours. I'm no Charlie Hill." She handed the lump of silver coins back to him.

"Are you saying you'll share in the work and the dangers but you won't share in the booty, if there is any?"

"All I want is to solve the mystery. That's more than enough for me."

"If you're not a partner, then what are you?"

"How about a friend, Jack? How about a friend, helping out?" Carrie said with a smile.

Chapter Seven

The clouds hanging over St. Thomas were numerous and obstinate, providing the island with a rare gray day and choppy waters that ruined all scuba-diving prospects.

But Carrie remained undaunted, much to Jack's mixed feelings. He couldn't deny the uneasiness he felt, watching her take over his space at the library with the authority of General Patton. In one day's time, not only did she clear the cobwebs from every nook and cranny of the room, but she completely revamped his personal card-catalog system and was now in the process of alphabetizing his news-clippings file.

Jack *liked* the place messy. He felt comfortable there. But each time he opened his mouth to voice his objections to Carrie's whirlwind organizational efforts, he had only to watch her for a moment and his objections melted away. She was having the time of her life.

She launched into every chore with enthusiasm, meticulously filing each card in its proper category, handling his aging books with reverence. Her hair was pulled back in a careless braid, and she bore a gray smudge on her nose, yet she glowed with something that transformed her into a stunning goddess.

She had relegated Jack to one corner of the room, where he used a window ledge for a desk. Whenever she ran across something promising, she handed it to him for further scrutiny.

"This isn't how I'd planned to spend my vacation," Carrie commented as she studied the brittle pages of a leather-bound volume. "But as long as it's raining, I can't think of anything I'd rather do."

Jack could think of several things he'd rather do, such as bundle up Carrie Bishop and take her to bed for a week or two. Theoretically, he agreed with Carrie; it would be foolish for them to share any further intimacy when in less than a week they would part company. Staying at arm's length was the sensible thing to do. But just the same . . .

She had her back to him, and Jack studied her with unhurried interest, from the top of her honey-blond head, down her slender neck, along the enticing curves of her back that tapered to a narrow waist and then flared gently down to her hips. His eyes finally settled on the firm, slender legs that had first attracted him to her.

He hadn't counted on his hunger for her overriding everything else in his mind, even his desire to unravel the *Laurel*'s mystery.

"Have you found anything in that file?" she asked, oblivious to his line of thought.

Jack closed the file labeled "Piracy" with a disgusted sigh. "Unfortunately, no. Nothing fits." Supposing Carrie's guess was right—that an undocumented pirate ship had been wrecked at the *Laurel* site—there were no accounts of piracy during the mid-eighteenth century that would dove-tail with the few facts they had.

Carrie reshelved the book she'd been studying and seated herself at Jack's desk. "Maybe we're going at this from the wrong angle. What do you know about the *Laurel*?"

Jack rummaged around until he came up with another manila folder containing all the facts he had on the small turn-of-the-century steamer. The information was slim.

"On July 12, 1899, a sailor by the name of Wilkes stumbled half-dead into Cruz Bay, St. John. He said his ship, a British mail packet called the *Laurel*, had crashed into a reef and everyone on board but him had drowned. He wouldn't reveal the exact location of the wreck, not until he had recovered his strength enough to help in the salvage operation. Unfortunately he died a short time later.

"The ship's remains were soon found, anyway. Divers recovered numerous items such as silverware, dishes and navigation equipment. The site was quickly picked clean. And that's about it."

"What was the ship doing here? Where did she come from?"

"That I don't know. I glanced briefly through the British maritime records and found no mention of her. But I don't have access to all the records, so that's not unusual."

"Unless . . ." Carrie's brows drew together thoughtfully.

"Unless what?"

"Unless the sailor's story was pure fabrication. Maybe your wreck isn't the *Laurel* at all."

Jack nodded thoughtfully, intrigued. "Go on."

"Maybe the ship was loaded with valuable artifacts. This sailor Wilkes could have made up a story about a mail boat called the *Laurel* because he didn't want anyone else to discover the ship's cargo. Then he died before he had a chance to salvage the valuable stuff for himself."

Jack had to admit that, as far-fetched as it sounded, Carrie's theory made more sense than anything he'd come up with. "If the ship did strike the reef several yards from where she eventually sank," he said, "it's possible that the valuable cargo spilled out, and that's why none was recovered. But where did this strange cargo come from?"

Carrie gave a defeated sigh. "We keep coming back to that question."

Jack rubbed his temples. "We've been at this an awfully long time. Why don't we knock off and get some dinner? I don't know about you, but my brain functions better if it has an occasional rest."

Carrie smiled sheepishly. "I'm being compulsive about this, aren't I?"

"'Driven' might be a more appropriate description." He softened the comment with a wink.

"I have an idea," said Carrie, the flash of inspiration in her eye. "I'll make it up to you by taking you out to dinner. Gifford drove me by this fabulous-looking restaurant called the Captain's Palace—"

Jack whistled. "It's pretty expensive."

"I can afford it. After all, you're going to save me a fortune on scuba lessons."

They had feasted on lobster and rack of lamb. Now, seated in the intimate confines of a booth overlooking the wind-roughened Atlantic, Carrie luxuriated in her own feeling of femininity. She'd all but forgotten the mystery of the *Laurel*.

Jack had hardly taken his eyes off her all evening. She wore the one real cocktail dress she'd brought with her, a blue-gray silk number that exactly matched her eyes. The dropped waist fanned into a full ruffle of a skirt that fluttered down to stop just above her knees.

She'd swept up her hair on one side with the sapphire comb, letting the rest of it hang loose. The curled ends tickled her bare shoulders every time she turned her head—which she did quite often, swiveling her attention between the breathtaking view and the dangerously debonair man who sat across from her.

She had never seen a man look so polished while still maintaining the aura of a swashbuckling pirate. His angular face was close-shaven, his mustache neatly trimmed, and his normally unruly hair was behaving, for once. His lightweight navy suit fit him to perfection, and the crisp white shirt shone stark against his deep tan. Carrie had to look away from time to time, just to stop her pulse from racing.

But she'd be leaving soon. She tried to dismiss the frantic thought, but it flitted through her consciousness like a troublesome gnat. She was as happy as she'd ever been, as she was likely to ever be, and the whole thing would be over in five days.

As she'd dressed this evening, she had tried to convince herself to apply for the library job. On the surface, it seemed like the answer to her prayers. But Grace Calhoun was right—the prospect of leaving her roots behind her was frightening. She might not have an exciting life in Des Moines, but it was comfortable. She had friends and family there who loved her. Des Moines was a known quantity.

What would her parents think if she up and moved to the Caribbean? They had been aghast at her decision to take a vacation there alone. They would probably faint dead away if she announced that she wanted to live there.

"You're frowning again," Jack said, absently stirring his coffee. "Last time I caught you frowning like that, you were thinking about us."

Carrie made an effort to smile. "Sorry, it was nothing. Oh, listen, the band's playing a rumba. You can finally give me that dance lesson you promised." She started to scoot out of the booth, but Jack reached across the table and took her hand.

"First there's something I have to tell you."

Carrie's heart fluttered as she gazed into Jack's jade-green eyes, which at the moment looked uncertain but earnest. What was he going to say? A million possibilities presented themselves in her mind. She shivered with anticipation.

"I can't rumba," he said, so quickly she wasn't sure she'd heard right.

"I beg your pardon?"

"I can't rumba, or tango. Not a step."

"You mean you lied?"

"Through my teeth. I would have said anything to get you to have dinner with me that first night."

His words thrilled her, but Carrie feigned indignation. "You took me out under false pretenses. I ought to report you to Detective Van Horn."

"He'd probably arrest me. He's been looking for an excuse. Then I'd be in jail, and you'd be without a bodyguard."

Carrie seemed to consider this possibility, though the reference to Jack as her bodyguard was a standing joke now. Claude had been laying low. His yacht hadn't been spotted in the harbor, and they had begun to believe that perhaps the Frenchman had moved on to more accommodating waters.

"Well, all right. I won't report you this time." She smiled wickedly. "But you'd better make good on your next promise."

"Oh, believe me, I will. I'm completely reformed." He lowered his voice to a velvet whisper. "If you'll walk with me on a deserted beach, I promise to kiss you until your toes curl."

Carrie shivered again, imagining that certain other parts of her anatomy would react, as well. Despite her fears for the future, she intended to give Jack every opportunity to make good on this promise.

They had forgone the scooter this evening in favor of more dignified transportation, but when they stepped outside the restaurant to hail a taxi for the ride home, they couldn't find one.

"Why don't you wait here while I try to get hold of Gifford?" Jack suggested. "He doesn't live far from here." They stepped inside the restaurant's front door. "I'll only be a minute."

Carrie nodded, then sank into one of the plushly upholstered chairs in the waiting area. One minute stretched into two, and two into five. Her dinner felt suddenly heavy in her stomach, and the atmosphere of the waiting area smotheringly oppressive. Abruptly she stood and stepped out the front door, where she was sure the bracing ocean breeze would perk her up.

She took two deep breaths and felt better immediately. It was on the third breath that she detected a familiar scent. She couldn't place it at first. It wasn't from the profusion of bright flowers that surrounded her, it was something else...

She finally made the connection, but too late. The scent was Claude Colline's expensive, heavy cologne. Suddenly a beefy arm caught her under the chin, and her arm was twisted painfully behind her back.

"Don't make a sound or I'll break something," a grating voice whispered in her ear. "I'm not playing games anymore. I want to know what Jack Harrington found and what he's looking for. I spent all day at that wreck site. There's nothing there, nothing!"

The voice sounded like Claude's, from what Carrie could remember. Yet there was something not quite right about it.

Her attacker tightened his grip on her arm until she thought it would be torn from its socket. "I won't ask again."

Carrie was too frightened to speak. But some part of her was calm enough to take action. Detaching herself from her fear, she remembered a self-defense technique she'd learned in a rape-prevention class at the hospital. With no idea whether it would work or not, she jabbed backward with her free elbow and raked a sharp heel down her attacker's shin, then ground her heel into his instep. She was rewarded with a grunt of pain. The man's grip loosened slightly, but that was all Carrie needed. She ducked away from him and bolted toward the door of the restaurant.

She didn't stop running until she found Jack, who was just returning from his phone call. She fell against him, relieved beyond words to have something solid and safe to hold on to.

"Carrie? What's wrong? What happened?"

"I jabbed him in the stomach and stamped on his foot and he let me go." She felt a strange sort of elation just before the room began to spin. Blackness started to close in, and she heard Jack speak from far away.

"Who let you go? Carrie?"

She awoke in a strange room, an office of some kind. She guessed she was still somewhere in the restaurant. Jack was sitting beside her, fanning her face with a menu and looking positively stricken. Gifford was there, too, his immense height more intimidating than ever from her vantage point.

"What happened?" She was astounded at the weakness of her voice.

"How do you feel?" Jack asked, ignoring her question. "Should I call a doctor?"

"No, I think I'm all right. As I said before, I tend to faint rather easily." She slowly pushed herself into a sitting position. Other than a sore arm, she felt okay. "Oh, now I remember. Claude Colline grabbed hold of me outside the restaurant . . ."

"Dear Lord," Jack muttered between clenched teeth.

"At least, I think it was Claude. I smelled his cologne, but I didn't see him. And his voice . . . there was something wrong with his voice. It sounded like Claude, and yet it didn't."

Jack had abandoned his fanning and was pacing the small office. "How could I have been so stupid? I never should have left you alone, not even for a minute. I let my guard down, and look what happens—"

"Do not blame yourself," Gifford offered.

"I shouldn't have walked outside alone," Carrie added.

"It was my fault, and you both know it," Jack said, savagely kicking the corner of the desk. He turned to Carrie and pointed a finger at her accusingly. "You've almost been killed twice, all because of the *Laurel*. Well, that's it. I'm giving up on it. Claude, whoever he is, can have whatever's there."

"Jack, no! We're not giving up. I wasn't 'almost killed,' not even close. Besides, Claude isn't going to leave us alone, not until you tell him exactly what to look for and where to find it. He's still on the wrong track." She recounted, as best she could remember, what her attacker had said during their brief struggle.

Jack took several deep breaths, trying to master his temper. "What happened to your shoe?"

Carrie looked down to discover that one foot was bare. "I guess I lost it when I ran away. Maybe it's still outside."

She ran impatient fingers through her thick hair, but her hand froze mid-gesture. "My sapphire comb is missing, too."

"I will look for it," Gifford offered as he made a quiet exit.

When they were alone, Jack sank onto the small sofa next to Carrie. "I didn't mean to lose my temper. The last thing you need right now is to listen to me ranting and raving."

Carrie smiled bravely. "I don't mind."

"You know I act that way because I'm concerned about you, right?"

She nodded.

Jack took her hand and rubbed his callused thumb absently over her knuckles. "I don't suppose you'd want to spend a few days of your vacation on another island, would you? There's a beautiful resort on Tortola—"

But Carrie was already shaking her head. "Not unless you come with me."

His soft, caring expression hardened. "I've got business to take care of."

Gifford returned, holding the shoe aloft triumphantly. "I'm afraid there's no sign of your comb, Miss."

Carrie shrugged. "It doesn't matter." She would miss the comb, but it was, after all, a legacy from Web. Maybe she was better off without it. She flexed her arm, wincing at the pain. "I'm all right now, let's get going. I think I'm going to need a long, hot bath."

Jack put a proprietary arm around her as they walked to Gifford's taxi. He assisted her into the back seat and climbed in after her, always touching her shoulder. Once they were settled, he never once loosened his grip on her hand, as if he were afraid she might disappear if he let her go.

Carrie had thought she might stay at the hotel that night. It made her edgy, sleeping so close to Jack without stepping over a line of intimacy they both wanted to cross. But after this last terrifying incident, she wasn't of a mind to be alone. When Jack directed Gifford to drive to his house, she voiced no objection. Gifford merely pursed his lips thoughtfully and said nothing.

After a few minutes of silence, Carrie decided that a little conversation would ease the slight tension that had descended on the taxi.

"What would it take," she asked, "to legally secure the wreck site and keep Claude away from it?"

Jack gave a short, humorless laugh. "I would have to get the university to underwrite salvaging the wreck. Then I could hire a fully equipped salvage boat—a bigger boat than mine, with heavier equipment—and a full-time staff of divers and archaeologists, not to mention round-the-clock security guards with big guns. Not even Claude would dare challenge me then."

"Isn't that what the university hired you to do? Salvage shipwrecks?"

"I was hired to locate and map shipwrecks. They wouldn't approve a full-fledged salvage operation without some kind of hard evidence that the wreck has historical merit. I'd need proof positive as to the identification of the ship and the source of the cargo."

"Excuse me," said Gifford. "You know how I love puzzles, Jack, but the answer to this one, really, is quite easy. The *Laurel* was a salvage vessel. That's where your strange cargo came from."

Jack and Carrie looked at each other, stunned at the simplicity of the answer. "Of course," said Jack. "How could I have not seen that?"

"I had the benefit of some evidence you don't have," said Gifford. "Many years ago, when I was hardly more than a boy, I found a diving bell buried in the sand near the *Laurel*. It's probably still there, though well covered with coral by now, I imagine."

"What's a diving bell?" Carrie asked.

"It's what the early divers sometimes used to get their oxygen supply, before the advent of scuba," Jack explained.

Carrie could barely contain her excitement. "All we have to do now is find out who in 1899 was doing a salvage operation of a mid-eighteenth-century shipwreck, right?"

Once again Jack had to smile at Carrie's naivete. "I'll be glad to turn you loose in my library. If you can come up with the answer to that one, I'll, um . . ."

"Careful, Jack," said Carrie, shaking a warning finger at him. "Remember, no promises you don't intend to keep."

Those words promptly reminded him of the moonlight walk on the beach and the toe-curling kiss he'd promised earlier that evening. He supposed that was out of the question now. Though Carrie had seemingly regained her good spirits, what she needed was to be tucked into bed with a warm glass of milk, not to trek around on some soggy, windy beach.

"There is a car following us," Gifford said calmly.

"What?" Jack turned. What looked like another taxi was a few car lengths behind. "Are you sure?"

"Positive. It's been behind us since we left the restaurant. I can lose it easy enough, but I fear your troubles won't be over."

"What do you mean?" Carrie asked.

"This Claude appears to be a ruthless man. If he has gone to the trouble to follow the two of you around, he knows where you live, Jack. You will not be safe there. But if I might make a suggestion?"

"Please," said Jack, almost queasy at the thought of exposing Carrie to any more danger.

"You can both stay with me. I have plenty of room and I would welcome the company."

Jack looked at Carrie. She nodded her approval. "Thanks, Gif, I think we'll take you up on your offer. But first, lose the tail. Then let's stop by my place so Carrie can get her things."

"No problem." Gifford pressed down on the gas pedal and the taxi lurched forward. After a few hair-raising turns, they left the pursuing car far behind.

It was after midnight when they arrived at Gifford's small frame house. Jack had always admired his friend's home. It was decorated with an amazing array of nautical gadgets both ancient and modern. An old-fashioned copper diving helmet rested in a corner of the living room. Huge jawbones, which Gifford claimed came from a shark that had tried to eat him, adorned one wall. A floor-to-ceiling bookcase was crammed with every manner of odds and ends, from old navigation equipment to rare seashells to a clipper ship in a bottle. Even the window in the front hall was in a nautical style. It was round like a porthole and framed by an old ship's wheel.

Jack looked on as Carrie's attention darted from one item to another. "This is a truly amazing collection," she told Gifford.

"I have even more in storage," he said, smiling proudly. "Now, my guests, please tell me—will you be requiring one bedroom or two?"

Jack tried not to laugh at the way his friend politely tackled the delicate subject, as if he were asking whether they drank tea or coffee. He caught Carrie's eye and winked before answering in kind. "Two, please."

Carrie convinced Jack to let her bring a couple of books from his office on board his boat the next morning. While he was teaching his scuba class, she would catch a few rays and work on narrowing the list of possible wrecks the *Laurel* had salvaged.

Jack had anchored the *Carrie* in the same calm cove where he had first instructed her in scuba basics. Now he and his small, trembling class stood in the shallows as Carrie lazed on deck. Her sunburn had mellowed to a golden tan, which she intended to deepen today. When she returned to Des Moines she wanted to look like she'd had fun in the sun. It wouldn't do if her friends knew she'd spent a great deal of her time on St. Thomas reading.

She opened the first book she'd brought, a comprehensive list of shipwrecks in the Western Hemisphere, ordered by area and date. She began writing the names of all the wrecks between 1749 and 1753 that were or might have been transporting gold and silver. Even after she eliminated those that stated "all cargo recovered," her list was formidable.

Dozens of ships, many of them carrying Spanish treasure, had sunk during hurricanes and other storms along the east coasts of the United States and South America, off the coast of Cuba and in and among the islands of the Caribbean. Sailing was not a terribly safe endeavor two hundred years ago, Carrie mused.

She meticulously recorded the available facts on these shipwrecks, then decided to take a break. She stood and stretched, glancing out at the water where she'd last seen the scuba class. They had disappeared under the surface, leaving her with an uncomfortable sensation of isolation.

Only one other boat was visible in the area, a large white vessel some distance out to sea. The craft looked as if it were heading toward the cove. Out of curiosity, Carrie picked up Jack's powerful binoculars and had a look.

The boat was beautiful, sleek, modern—and somehow sinister. Carrie kept the binoculars trained on the man at the helm as the boat drew closer. It had to be Claude. And here she was, alone for all practical purposes, defenseless.

She'd seen a spear gun below. Quickly, she scurried through the hatch, located the gun and brought it on deck. She hadn't the slightest idea how to use it, but perhaps the mere sight of the weapon would keep Claude at a distance.

When she raised the binoculars again, she discovered that the man at the helm was looking at her through a telescope. Carrie waved uncertainly, holding tight to the spear gun.

The man at the helm raised his arm, but instead of waving he made an obscene gesture. Yes, that had to be Claude. Abruptly, the yacht turned hard to port and was soon sailing in the opposite direction. Carrie could just make out the boat's name: *Touché*. Shaking, she sank onto the nearest bench.

The first splashes from the diving platform a few minutes later signaled that the divers were returning. Carrie had put the spear gun back in place, and now she put her books away as well, to protect them from being dripped on by the scuba class.

She assisted the students one by one, helping them shed their tanks, masks, weight belts and flippers as they chattered about the amazing things they'd seen during their dive.

Jack was the last to board. His eyes immediately sought out Carrie.

Though still a bit shaken, she smiled reassuringly at him, determined not to make a big thing of the incident with Claude. Jack would only blame himself for letting her out of his sight again.

"Did you get some reading done?" he asked her, leaning toward her to sneak a kiss.

"Yes, and I have a list of wrecks as long as your arm. I plan to research them as soon as you let me into your library." Though Jack obviously needed no help with his diving equipment, she released the clasp on his weight belt and removed it, letting her hands linger along his ribs.

"Watch where you touch, lady, or you'll find yourself part of an undignified display right in front of all these people."

Carrie retreated to a safe distance, focusing her attention on the students and helping them return their equipment to the proper areas.

"You haven't chickened out of diving this afternoon, have you, Carrie?" Jack was behind her, his broad hands spanning her narrow waist.

"We need to reconsider our plans," she said, thinking about Claude. "I'm not sure we'd be safe."

"There won't be any more problems with the tanks—"

"I'm not talking about the tanks. See that boat out there?" She pointed to the retreating *Touché*, now not much more than a dot on the horizon.

"What about it?"

She turned to face him and lowered her voice to a whisper, not wanting the scuba students to hear. "That's Claude's yacht. He's keeping tabs on us. He won't come close enough to cause trouble if he knows someone is on the boat who can identify him or call for help on the radio. But if we were both underwater, with the *Carrie* unguarded..."

Jack's mouth twisted grimly. "I see what you mean."

"If there was a third person we could bring along to watch the boat—what about Gifford?"

"I feel we've imposed on him enough," said Jack.

"But he loves this intrigue stuff," Carrie objected. "We could pay him for the afternoon."

Jack reluctantly agreed, though he still wished he could convince Carrie to spirit herself away to someplace safer until this trouble had a chance to blow over. But she had a barrage of sensible arguments that kept her here, and no amount of persuasion on his part would change her mind.

Four more days. If he could just keep her safe for that long, she'd be on a plane for the States and out of harm's way. He pictured the scene—Carrie stepping onto the plane, waving at him from the window. Instead of relief, the image produced a flood of mixed feelings in Jack.

"What's wrong?" said Carrie. "You look as if you just took a bite of a sour apple."

Chapter Eight

It was when she was diving on a sunny afternoon two days later that Carrie caught her first glimpse of gold under the sea. It was a mere shimmer in the sand, and she thought at first the sun was playing tricks on her eyes.

She had spent the better part of two days underwater with Jack. She was actually beginning to feel relaxed and at home with a mask strapped to her face and a regulator in her mouth. The tank was feeling less cumbersome all the time.

She had learned to identify numerous species of bright tropical fish and had thrilled at the sight of a graceful manta ray gliding silently by her not ten feet away.

On the negative side, neither she nor Jack had discovered any more artifacts. They had systematically covered the area around their previous finds, fanning away the sand with paddles. It wasn't the most effective means of surveying, Jack had explained. If he hadn't been worried about Claude, he would have hooked up a blaster to the boat's prop and really given the area a once-over. He also would have been drawing a grid on the sea floor with stakes and strings, but it would be too easy for Claude to stumble across it. So they ambled along with paddles, hoping to get lucky.

Carrie's heart pounded as the gold winked at her, inviting her for a closer look. It seemed to disappear as she closed in, but with a small wave of her paddle the sand stirred, revealing a cylinder of gold encrusted with gemstones. In her excitement she started to swim toward Jack, then realized she might lose her place. She returned to the spot and waited a few moments until Jack looked up from his own work; then she signaled frantically.

He was at her side instantly. She pointed to the object. He saw it, and she knew that mentally he was jumping up and down, hugging her. He plucked it from the sand, and together they studied it.

The object turned out to be the handle of a dagger, its blade long disintegrated. Carrie could hardly bear to take her eyes off its sparkling surface, studded with emeralds and rubies. Even the bright underwater world paled in comparison to the dagger's beauty.

It was several minutes later that Carrie thought to look at her air gauge. She nudged Jack and pointed to it, and he nodded, placing the dagger handle in his goody bag. They had just enough air left to swim back to the boat.

Gifford, who was casting a lazy fishing line into the water while keeping an eye on the *Carrie*, fairly crowed when the divers emerged with the newfound artifact. "In all my days as a diver," he declared, examining the dagger, "I have never seen such a magnificent thing brought up from the sea. Jack, my friend, you truly are onto something significant."

Jack grinned unabashedly, but then his features clouded over in a thoughtful expression. "If only the university shared your sentiments," he commented, slipping his tank off. "The head of the marine archaeology department is definitely intrigued with my findings so far. He's handling the paperwork for the grant application, but he tells me the project won't be approved without more proof that something's really down there."

"You mean this isn't proof enough?" Carrie asked, gazing at the extravagant object in Gifford's hand.

Jack's grin returned. "Today's find certainly won't hurt my chances. But we're talking a big commitment on the part of the university. They'll want to know *exactly* what's down there." He turned his attention to Gifford. "Any trouble while we were gone?"

"Not exactly, but I did receive a radio message for you. The sender did not leave his name, but there was no need. He said, and I quote, 'Tell Monsieur Harrington his luck is running out.'"

Though the late afternoon sun was warm, Carrie felt a chill that ran all the way to her bones. Claude certainly had a flair for intimidation. Even when he was miles away, he was able to reach long, icy fingers to touch them. She searched deeply inside herself for some confidence. "He's just trying to unnerve us. What else can he do that he hasn't already tried?"

Jack's face hardened. "There's a hell of a lot he can do. We can't let down our guard, any of us. Not for a minute."

"Do we have time for another dive today?" Carrie asked. seeking to rid herself of the crawly sensations that made her shiver.

Jack traced his index finger along the red creases in Carrie's forehead, nose and cheeks caused by her mask. "I don't think so. You've already been down twice today, and I've been down three times. That's enough bodily stress for one day. Maybe we should have another go-around at the library instead."

She nodded her agreement. "I'll fix an early dinner when we get back—I'll fry up that chicken we bought yesterday. Then we'll be ready to hit the books."

Carrie's stomach was full and her mind hungry for information as she and Jack arrived at the library three hours later. They had made slow but steady progress on the list of shipwrecks she had compiled two days ago, having eliminated several possibilities.

A stack of facsimile transmissions from the Library of Congress was waiting for them when they entered Jack's office. Carrie went to work on the documents immediately, devouring them and taking notes as fast as her hand could move.

She was scanning one, an old clipping from a Norfolk, Virginia, newspaper, when the solution to their mystery hit her like a shot between the eyes.

"Jack!" she shrieked. "Come quick, I think I've found it."

She tried to hold the document steady as Jack read over her shoulder, but her hand trembled with her excitement. He finally had to pull the paper away from her and lay it flat on the desk so they both could read the tiny, blurred print.

The date was August 1, 1899. The story told of a salvage operation taking place on the Virginia coast. Seven ships of the New Spain Flotilla of Captain General Juan Manuel de Bonilla had been lost off the coast of North Carolina and Virginia during a hurricane in 1750. The Spaniards and British had recovered most of the treasure, but the gold in one of the ships, the *San Salvador*, hadn't been relocated until 1899.

At the news of the discovery, several British and American salvage vessels rushed to the site and recovered a great deal of gold. But one of the salvage ships, the *Constantine*, met up with a storm on the way back to England, the newspaper reported. All of its crew and cargo were lost.

"So," said Jack, his shaking voice a testimony to his own excitement. "You think the *Constantine* and the *Laurel* are one and the same? That a crooked captain took advantage of a storm and headed for the Virgin Islands with a stolen shipload of gold, hoping he and his crew would be given up for sunk?"

"You have to admit it all fits," said Carrie. "But how do we go about proving this theory?"

He smiled triumphantly. "We make a phone call to Seville, Spain."

"No kidding? What's there?"

"The Archives of the Indies, containing all the old Spanish shipping records. I have a friend there who can get in and find the cargo manifest for the *San Salvador*. He can translate it and send it to us via computer modem. Once we have a list of the cargo, we see if the things we've found match up. If we get a good enough match..." He shrugged with deceptive casualness.

"That's it? We have our proof?" She stared at him, hardly daring to believe they were so close. Jack, too, looked as if he was afraid to believe they'd found the answer.

Suddenly the elation bubbled up through Jack's cautious facade. He began to smile widely, then laugh out loud. He stood swiftly, upsetting a foot-high stack of papers at his elbow in the process. The papers slid to the floor in a noisy avalanche as Jack pulled Carrie to him and swung her around.

She laughed and shrieked for him to put her down, but as far as she was concerned he could swing her all he wanted.

This was the moment she'd been waiting for—the moment Jack's bitterness over the past melted away as the joy of discovery enveloped him. She knew she would carry his smile, his laughter and his triumph with her the rest of her life.

When Jack finally put her down, he didn't release her. His smile faded and his eyes darkened with another emotion, one Carrie couldn't quite read. But suddenly it was as if he had taken all the energy from his elation and channeled it into something else, something intense—and aimed right at her.

She absorbed that energy, as if she were a receiver tuned to Jack's frequency. It filled every part of her with warmth.

Their lips met hungrily. His tongue teased and explored her mouth, and the warmth that filled her expanded even further, overflowing, cascading over her like rays of sunshine. An exquisite pressure began to build deep inside Carrie as Jack loosened the clip that held her ponytail. She felt the waves of hair come free, felt Jack's fingers combing gently through the strands, as delicately as if he were handling spun silk.

Jack inhaled, forever captivated by Carrie's unique scent. He trailed kisses along her jaw, nibbled her earlobe, buried his face in her glorious hair. Unconsciously one of his hands had wandered over her shoulder and down to cup her breast. His thumb massaged her nipple through the thin cotton of her shirt. He felt the peak grow hard beneath his hand.

He pulled her closer until they were thigh to thigh, hip to hip. God, how he wanted her. The fierceness of his desire was as exciting as it was unpredictable.

Carrie's knees wobbled. The evidence of Jack's desire was plain, and her answering need just as intense. It felt right and good for her to be with this man. But in the back of her mind, nagging thoughts haunted her. *I'll be gone in two days. I'll never see him again. I have no future with Jack.*

Live for the moment, Carrie Bishop! an inner voice urged.

But that's not really my way of doing things, she argued. In the week she'd been on the island, she'd learned that about herself. She craved excitement and adventure, and she'd gotten both, but she still thought in terms of actions and consequences. A transient affair with Jack just wasn't in her.

Why does it have to be temporary? the inner voice questioned again. *What happened to that woman who wanted to be the maker of her own destiny?*

"Carrie, what's wrong?" Jack whispered.

"Hmm?" Her mind was suddenly teeming with decisions to be made.

"You stiffened up like a two-by-four. Did I hurt you? Did I scare you?"

The concern in his voice nearly brought tears to her eyes. She smiled reassuringly. *No, my dear Jack, you didn't hurt me and you didn't scare me. You woke me up, is what you did.* She took both his hands and clasped them in hers. "There's a time and a place for everything," she said.

He smiled wistfully. "I know. And this isn't it."

She brought her hand to his face, stroking it softly, feathering the corner of his mustache with her thumb. Dear Lord, she couldn't possibly leave him.

"I wish there was more time," he said, cradling her head against the hollow of his shoulder. "If I'd known how things between us would turn out . . ."

"You would have stayed miles away from me," Carrie finished for him.

"No, that's not true at all. I wouldn't give up the time we've had together for anything."

That was exactly what Carrie needed to hear.

A few minutes later, as they headed out of the library, she decided the sooner she got the ball rolling the better. There wasn't much time left in which to implement her new plan.

"Just a minute, I want to talk to Grace," she said. The tone of her voice and her body language communicated one additional word: *privately*. Jack hung back obligingly as Carrie approached the circulation desk, where Grace Calhoun was sorting through returned books.

Grace looked up and gave a welcoming smile. "Hi, Carrie. You two have been holed up in that back office so long I was wondering if you'd taken up permanent residence. Glad to see you've come out for some fresh air."

"Have you filled the librarian job yet?" Carrie asked without preamble.

"No." Grace's plucked brows made arches above her hazel eyes. "Dare I hope you're interested?"

"I'm more than interested. I want it. It took thirty years, but I've finally found a place that feels like home, and I intend to stay here. Should I fill out an application? Will you want to schedule a formal interview?"

"Oh, gracious, no. You're hired. When can you start?"

Carrie blinked a couple of times, hardly able to believe things were happening so fast. "How about Monday morning?"

"Fine. I'll see you at eight o'clock." They shook hands, and the deed was done.

Carrie, still slightly stunned, walked slowly back to where Jack waited for her. In the span of less than a minute she'd started a process that was going to change her whole life.

"I want to pick up just a couple of souvenirs," Carrie argued the next morning. "Gifford will look after me."

Jack couldn't believe his ears. Why would Carrie want to go shopping, now of all times? They were so close to solving their mystery he could taste it. They'd gotten up at three o'clock that morning to make the phone call to his friend Emil in Seville, and they were hoping to receive the translated cargo manifest later in the day.

"If you'll wait till after my class, I'll go with you," he reasoned.

But this, apparently, wasn't a satisfactory alternative to Carrie. She didn't argue, though. She merely looked at him with those soulful gray-blue eyes. Why did he have the feeling there was something she wasn't telling him?

Jack sighed, knowing he was defeated. He couldn't deny the woman anything. "I don't have to tell you to watch out, do I?"

"You know I'll be careful. And Gifford wouldn't let anything happen to me."

Jack still worried about her, of course. He went through the motions during his class, all of which were second nature to him now, but his thoughts were constantly on Carrie. He'd been crazy to let her out of his sight. Every time he did, something awful happened. Gifford was smart and trustworthy, but he was only an old man, after all. A million terrible fates could befall those two.

Jack's worrying intensified when Carrie was not waiting for him at the hotel pier after the class was over. He checked in the lobby for messages, but there were none. Myra hadn't seen Carrie, either. Jack was close to frothing at the mouth by the time he returned to the pier. Then relief flooded over him as he spied Carrie sitting on the edge of the dock, taking pictures of Gifford wading on the beach.

She looked just as she had the day he met her. He'd thought her an innocent farm girl that day, he remembered, with the face of an angel. Now that he knew her, he'd discovered she was less of an angel than she looked. Right now he wanted to shake her until her teeth rattled.

"Carrie Bishop, I'm going to handcuff you to me," he threatened, hauling her to her feet and crushing her against him in a bear hug. "Where have you been? You had me worried half sick."

"Where have *you* been?" she countered sweetly, not at all put off by his caveman display. "I've been waiting on the dock almost ten minutes."

Ah, well, what did it matter now? Jack thought. She was safe. He'd put her under lock and key to keep her that way, if he had to. And tomorrow she'd be away from this pirate's den.

"Are we diving this afternoon?" Carrie asked.

Jack didn't want to take her diving. Too many things could happen. "Let's eat first. Then we probably should check the computer at the library, see if Emil's come up with that cargo manifest. Did you get your shopping done?"

"My what?"

"Shopping," he repeated. For someone who was so intent on it this morning, the subject certainly had slipped her mind in a hurry.

"Oh. Yes, all done." Carrie smiled mysteriously.

The small computer room at the library was quiet except for the periodic whir of the mainframe and the clicking of the keys as Jack's fingers moved over them. Breathless, Carrie watched the terminal screen as the transmission from Seville, Spain, appeared, line by agonizingly slow line.

"Greetings, my friend Juan," it began.

"Juan?" Carrie raised one questioning eyebrow at Jack. He shrugged. "That's what Emil calls me."

"The cargo manifest you requested, from the *San Salvador*, lost in 1750, was easy enough to find. Below is a complete listing of the cargo. But I understand the treasure was salvaged ninety years ago. Hope this helps, anyway—whatever you're doing. Emil.''

As the list began to appear on the screen, neither Carrie nor Jack uttered a word. Then, less than a minute later, the transmission abruptly stopped.

Jack punched a couple of keys, but no more words appeared.

''That can't be all of it,'' he said, his voice barely a whisper.

''No, look, there's more,'' Carrie said, but it was only Emil's sign-off code. She looked at Jack then. His face had tensed into lines of frustration, and she could understand why. The manifest had mentioned silver wedges and gold specie, but no coins. It had mentioned K'ang Hsi china, gold rings with emeralds and diamonds, a gold-plated sea horse with rubies for eyes and a diamond coiled in its tail. There were dozens of items of jewelry—but no jeweled daggers, no rosaries.

Carrie slowly released the breath she'd been holding. ''I feel like a dog that's been barking up the wrong tree,'' she said. ''Is there any chance the cargo manifest is wrong?''

''There's a chance.... Sometimes cargo wasn't recorded correctly.''

''But do you think that's the case here?''

Jack shook his head. ''If even one item matched up, I'd be more hopeful. But as it is...''

''Then the *Laurel* isn't really the *Constantine* after all. Damn! I was so sure, as if the proof were already right there in my hand. Well, we'll just have to keep looking.''

''The answer could take months—years. I don't have that long.''

''I'll help. We can't give up now.''

"You forget, your plane leaves in less than twenty-four hours." He looked away from her as he said this, and his voice shook ever so slightly. Carrie had been waiting for the right time to tell him of her decision to stay on the island. This was as good a time as any.

"No, my plane doesn't leave tomorrow."

"Tomorrow's Sunday, right?"

"I'm not leaving at all, Jack. I returned my plane ticket this morning when I was out with Gifford. I called Des Moines and arranged to have everything moved out of my apartment and sold or shipped here. I'm having my banks close my accounts and wire me the money. My sister is going to buy my car—"

"Wait a minute! Hold up! You can't just pick up and move here on a whim."

"It's no whim," she said quietly, trying to keep the panic out of her voice. "I've thought about it long and hard. And it's already done." This wasn't the reaction she'd anticipated from Jack, not at all.

"Then you can just *un*do it. I want you on that plane tomorrow, do you hear me?"

Carrie heard, all right. She also heard her whole world, the one she'd been so carefully constructing, crashing into a million pieces all around her.

Jack didn't want her here.

How could she have been so completely wrong about their relationship? She'd assumed that just because she wanted to remain with him, he felt the same way. In fact, she would have bet her right arm and left leg that that had been the case. Apparently she wasn't as good a judge of the situation as she'd believed.

Hot tears threatened behind her eyes. Having Jack witness the indignity of her crying would just ice the miserable cake, wouldn't it? she thought. "Excuse me," she said in a shaky voice, "I need to visit the ladies' room." She picked up her purse and exited the computer room, but instead of heading for the lavatory, she left the library.

Carrie had no clear idea of where she was going, except that she knew she had to get as far away from Jack as possible. She hitched a ride into town with a student she'd often seen studying in the library. From town she caught a taxi to the hotel. She'd held onto her room there even though she was staying at Gifford's.

Myra looked up as Carrie strode through the lobby. Somehow Carrie summoned a stiff smile and a curt wave, though she never broke stride. She wasn't in the mood for a chat just now. She needed some time to herself, time to figure out what she was going to do with her life.

Maker of her own destiny? Ha! she thought with a self-deprecating sigh as she walked down the hall toward her room.

Succumbing to habit, she opened the door cautiously to be sure she'd had no surprise visitors. But all looked as she'd left it. After slamming the door behind her, she retrieved her empty suitcases from beneath the bed and methodically began to fill them with her clothes and souvenirs. She'd go home, that was what she'd do. None of the arrangements she'd made were irreversible. She hadn't put down a deposit on an apartment here yet; Gifford had offered to let her stay in his guest room until she made other arrangements.

She'd simply buy another plane ticket and leave—today, now.

A soft knock on the door interrupted her thoughts. *Don't let it be Jack,* she pleaded silently. *I don't want to face him again.*

"Carrie, honey, it's me, Myra."

Relieved, Carrie opened the door. Myra she could handle.

"My dear girl, whatever is wrong?" Myra asked, her dark eyes full of concern. "When I see one Bobbsey twin without the other, I know something is amiss. Trouble in paradise?"

"I'll say," Carrie retorted. She continued to stuff things into her suitcases helter-skelter, muttering more to herself than Myra. "Sure, hanging out with Carrie the tourist is fine, a pleasant, *temporary* diversion. But God forbid I should offer him something long-term, something lasting."

"I assume you mean Jack," Myra said, sitting on the edge of the bed and helping herself to the mint the maid had left on Carrie's pillow. "What's he done wrong?"

"What can I say, Myra? You were right. You warned me that nothing was as important to him as his treasure hunting, and you were right. To him I was nothing but a—"

"Hold on a minute," Myra interrupted. "Don't make any hasty conclusions. I'm not so sure I was right. In fact, I was under the distinct impression that you were more than a little special to Jack."

"So was I. But he knew I'd be leaving. He didn't have to worry about any sticky entanglements. You should have seen his reaction when I mentioned that I was staying here permanently—"

"You're staying?"

"I was. I thought Jack would be happy when I told him. Instead he was horrified." Carrie saw Myra's disbelieving expression. "No kidding," she added. "I think he was counting the hours until he could be rid of me."

Myra continued to look puzzled. "I just can't believe that about Jack. He may not be perfect, but he is honest. He doesn't play games, Carrie. You must be mistaken."

If only she were, Carrie thought. "Weren't you dead set against any kind of romance between Jack and me?" she asked Myra. "You even warned us away from each other."

"I was, at first," Myra admitted. "But I've seen you together enough to realize I was wrong. You two make a heck of team."

Carrie shook her head. "I thought so too, but—"

The phone's ring interrupted her. She walked toward it, stared at it, almost answered it, then didn't.

Myra looked at her disapprovingly. "So what's all this packing about?"

"I'm catching the first plane out of here. I've overstayed my welcome."

"Oh, Carrie, don't. Wait at least another day. I'm sure you can work things out."

Carrie zipped up her bulging suitcases. "Is there any problem with checking out of the hotel one day early?"

Myra crossed her arms over her chest, clearly put out that Carrie wasn't taking her advice. "No, I suppose not. Here, I thought you might want these. I charged them to your bill." She reached into the pocket of her linen jacket and pulled out three fat red-and-yellow envelopes—the photos from the film Carrie had dropped off at the hotel drugstore yesterday.

Carrie thanked Myra and dropped the photos into her purse. She'd look at them later.

At the front desk she retrieved the remainder of her traveler's checks from the hotel safe and paid her bill. Then, with a suitcase in each hand, she thanked Myra as warmly as she knew how before heading out the massive glass front doors.

She waved to one of the bellhops. "I need a taxi, please," she called to him.

"Should be one coming around any time," he answered. So she sat on the low wall in front of the hotel and waited.

It was a warm eighty degrees outside, freshened by a light sea breeze. Carrie turned her face up to the sun and wondered what the temperature was right now in Des Moines. Maybe there was snow on the ground. Maybe they'd have a white Christmas. The thought didn't cheer her up in the least.

No taxi in sight. Absently, Carrie reached into her purse where she'd stashed the snapshots. The first envelope contained her most recent photos, including a few of Gifford cavorting in the shallows at the hotel pier. He'd loosened up a little in the past couple of days. She would truly miss him.

She glanced over the other photos of panoramic views, of local children, historic sites, of yellow hibiscus and scarlet frangipani in full bloom. The colors were so vivid in the Caribbean, Carrie mused. Everything was so full of life here. Damn it, she loved it. She didn't want to leave, not really.

Then why was she leaving? Because of Jack, of course. But if she based all her decisions on Jack's feelings, wouldn't she be falling back into the very pattern of dependency she'd worked so hard to obliterate? What about Carrie Bishop's feelings? Did she or did she not want to live on St. Thomas?

She did, and by God she'd do it, with or without Jack Harrington's support. The island felt like home to her already. She knew she could be content here, though without Jack she wasn't sure she could be completely happy anywhere.

The last batch of photos were all a hazy blue. They were from her first roll of film, she realized, the one that had received a salt-water dunking the day she'd first met Jack. She uncovered the only photo she had of Jack, the one she'd taken right after he'd retrieved the camera from a bed of seaweed. He was treading water, his mask and snorkel pushed up on his forehead, and smiling wickedly.

That's how she wanted to think of him—not angry, with the taste of a bad surprise in his mouth, as she'd seen him last.

A shadow fell over her. She looked up to see that a late-model luxury car had pulled up beside her.

"Taxi, lady?" the driver asked, hopping out to get her bags. She started to tell him no, that she'd changed her mind and was staying after all, but the sight of Jack's scooter barreling toward the hotel caused her to reconsider. She didn't want to face him yet, and if she didn't make a quick getaway she'd have no choice. He'd run right into her.

She nodded, and the taxi driver quickly put her bags in the trunk. She'd have him take her to Gifford's.

He opened the back door of the silver car for her. Her eyes still following Jack, she climbed in. It was only as the door slammed beside her that she realized she wasn't alone in the back seat. Claude Colline sat next to her, a small revolver pointed at her heart.

Chapter Nine

Carrie stifled her scream. Hysteria would be no help. Her eyes darted out the window as the car pulled away from the curb. Had Jack seen her? No, he was parking his scooter in a tow-away zone, his attention focused on the hotel's front door. If only he'd arrived a moment sooner!

She'd been so upset after running away from Jack that she'd all but forgotten the danger of traveling on her own. Now her carelessness was paying her back in a big way.

"You're so quiet, Miss Bishop," said Claude, never moving the gun an inch. "You don't have anything to say to me?"

If she said anything, it would be to lash out angrily, and Carrie knew it wouldn't be wise to provoke this crazy, violent man. She remained silent, ignoring Claude and taking stock of the other occupants of the car. The bland-faced driver seemed unimpressed by the rude display going on in the back seat. Carrie was not surprised to see that Jolly was also in the front, his head twisted around to watch the proceedings. His eyes were wide, glued to the ugly snub-nosed weapon clenched in Claude's hand.

"Nice company you keep, Roger," she said to the boy.

He shifted his gaze from the gun to her, his eyes wide with fear. "But I didn't know anything like this was—"

"Quiet, Jolly," said Claude, his tone inviting no argument. "Turn around and watch the road."

Jolly did.

But Carrie hadn't missed the note of insecurity in Claude's voice—or the momentary slipping of his French accent. Of course! Something about his voice had bothered her all along. The accent was phony. She'd thought the man who accosted her outside the restaurant had sounded like Claude, and yet not quite. Now she knew what had caused her confusion. In his frustration and fury at the time, the accent had all but disappeared.

So the man was only impersonating a Frenchman. Then who was he in reality?

Claude Colline. Colline. Didn't that word mean something in English? She searched her memory for those long-ago French classes from college. Meadow? Valley? Hill, that was it.

Involuntarily she gasped. *Charlie Hill*.

"Something wrong?" Claude asked, smiling wolfishly.

Carrie was so appalled by the man's audacity that prudence was the last thing on her mind. "I guess you weren't content stealing just one treasure from Jack," she blurted out.

"I have no idea what you're talking about," he said. But she could see by the brief expression of panic that crossed Claude's—Charlie's—face that she'd guessed right. His hand gripped the gun so tightly that his knuckles turned white.

"You know exactly what I'm talking about, Charlie. You took away a shipwreck that belonged to Jack and you made yourself a millionaire. But that wasn't enough, was it? How long have you been following him, spying on him, waiting for him to find something else you could take away—"

"That's enough!" he exploded. His face had turned an unhealthy shade of red, and his breathing was labored. "So, you figured it out, smart girl. But if you were really smart you would have kept your mouth shut. I wasn't planning to hurt you, you know. I just wanted to scare you into telling me about Jack's latest find. But the fact that you know who I am complicates matters." He scowled, then continued.

"I didn't care if you implicated Claude Colline in any sort of criminal misdeed. His identity was easy enough to slip out of, if things got too hot. Change the name and the registration numbers on my boat, switch to a different set of credit cards, drop the accent and *voilà*, no more Claude. But to identify Charlie Hill as the culprit, that's another matter altogether. In fact, Miss Bishop, your newfound knowledge, combined with what Jack knows of me, poses a very great threat to my well-being..." He grew pensive as he stared out the window, but the gun's deadly aim never changed.

"Where is she?" Jack bellowed at Myra in the hotel lobby. Several heads turned his way.

"Jack, please. Don't cause an uproar."

"She's not at Gifford's," he continued in a more controlled voice. "She must be here."

"Even if I knew where she was, I wouldn't tell you," Myra retorted. "Shame on you, upsetting that sweet girl like that. Leading her on, making her think she was something special—"

"She *is* something special. But do you know what that crazy little fool wanted to do? She wanted to stay here."

"Imagine that," said Myra, her sarcasm plain. "She wanted to live in a tropical paradise and be near the man she loves."

Jack's heart skipped a beat. "Did she say that?"

"Not in so many words. But it's easy to see what's in the girl's eyes as plain as day. She made a very difficult decision, to give up her home and family and friends so she could stay here with you. She anticipated that you would be pleased. And when she told you, how did you react?"

Jack sank into the nearest chair. "Not very well, I'm afraid."

"The poor girl thinks you couldn't wait to get rid of her."

Jack banged his fist on Myra's desk. "That's not it at all! I couldn't wait to get her on a plane to safety. Her life is in jeopardy here. As soon as the danger was past I would have asked her to come back. Or I would have gone to her. I'm crazy about Carrie."

"Did you tell her any of that?"

Jack struggled to remember. "Not exactly. I was so surprised by what she told me, I said the first thing that came to mind...." He tried to recall the exact words. When he did, he groaned. "I must have sounded like a jerk."

"You didn't win any awards as a smooth talker, that's for sure."

"C'mon, Myra, where is she? I can straighten this out if I can just talk to her."

Myra hesitated, then relented. "She's going to be on the first plane home. She left only a few minutes ago, so maybe you can catch her."

On the first plane home, Jack thought. The good news was she'd be safe. The bad news was he might never see her again.

"Jack, aren't you going after her?"

He stood slowly. "Yes I . . . No. Better to leave her where she is. And cancel all my scuba classes for the next few days, would you?"

Myra stammered objections after him as he strode away.

Jack's thoughts returned to when he'd last seen Carrie, at the library. While waiting for her to return from the ladies' room, he'd studied that cargo manifest for many long minutes. And he'd decided that he wouldn't give up on the *Constantine* theory, not until he'd recovered more artifacts. The handful of things found so far just wasn't enough on which to base a conclusion.

He'd felt excited and hopeful again—until he'd realized that Carrie wasn't coming back. Then all he could think about was finding her.

Now that he knew she was on her way to safety, he had only one immediate objective. He would dive at the wreck site every day, morning and afternoon, and spend his nights at the library until he found proof, one way or another, of the shipwreck's identity. With that proof in hand, the university would have to sanction the salvage project and grant him the support—and the protection—to insure that no one else would lay claim to the wreck.

Claude Colline would have to steal someone else's treasure; he'd no longer be able to threaten Jack. And Jack would be free to bring Carrie back here where she belonged—with him.

Carrie surveyed the luxurious salon aboard the *Touché*, her mind searching for some means of escape. The odds of overpowering her captors looked hopeless. The yacht was anchored far away from any other boats, so the chances of her signaling for help were remote. Carrie was not a strong swimmer, so she didn't dare try anything heroic, such as jumping overboard and heading for shore. There didn't appear to be anyone aboard the small yacht who could help her.

"Sit," Charlie commanded Carrie.

She did, on the edge of a soft, L-shaped sofa. Jolly hung back, watching, and the chauffeur went to a bar to mix himself and Charlie drinks.

Recognizing her powerlessness in the face of the gun, Carrie occupied herself by studying her companions, trying to figure out what motivated each one. The more she knew about her captors, she figured, the better chance she would have of outwitting them.

She already knew what motivated Charlie Hill: unspeakable greed. And maybe the desire to outwit the worthy opponent he saw in Jack.

It was hard to tell anything about the other man. His face remained expressionless, his eyes never meeting anyone's. Other than when he'd asked her if she needed a taxi, she hadn't heard him speak.

Then there was Jolly Roger. She stared pointedly at him, but he averted his eyes. He looked definitely uncomfortable. Carrie sensed that he heartily disapproved of what was going on here, and that, given half a chance, he might come to her aid. That notion gave her a sliver of hope.

"I hadn't planned on actually kidnapping you," Charlie said, taking a seat in a fat armchair facing her, holding the gun in a casual grip. "But now that you're here, there are a few ways I can take advantage of the situation. Why don't you save us both some trouble and tell me what Jack's onto and exactly where he found it?"

Carrie remained stubbornly silent.

"Come on, now. You can't pretend it isn't something grand. I have the comb, remember? Frankly I was surprised Jack had given you such a valuable piece. He's getting sentimental in his old age."

"Wait a minute—you think the sapphire comb—" She laughed out loud.

"Why else do you think I've been following you?"

She longed to tell him the comb was a fake and wipe that superior smile off Claude's face. But she held her tongue.

Claude's mouth formed a grim crease in his face. "All right, I gave you your chance. Maybe your boyfriend will be a little more cooperative once he figures out he's misplaced you."

The last thing Carrie wanted was to be used as a weapon against Jack. She mustered what little theatrical ability she had so as to appear indifferent. "I doubt he'll care one way or another. We were through, anyway. I was on my way to the airport."

Charlie eyed her with new interest. "He gave you the boot, huh? You thought you were going to get a share of that treasure, and instead you got a one-way ticket back to Iowa. Pity."

She shrugged sullenly.

"Well, I think it's time me and my old pal Jack had a reunion. Any idea where I might find him? I think he still might be persuaded to loosen up his tongue a bit. Even if he's through with you, I doubt he'd want to see you hurt."

Carrie had no doubt Charlie was right on that score. Though Jack might not like the idea of a long-term relationship, she couldn't bring herself to believe he didn't care about her, at least a little. "You might find him at the library," she offered, confident that Jack was not there.

Quickly Charlie tied Carrie's wrists together. Then, none too gently, he shoved her into a metal utility closet and locked the door. She could see nothing, but she could hear muffled voices.

"Keep an eye on her, Jolly. Make sure she stays put."

"Yes, sir."

"And quit looking at me like that. We're about to latch onto that treasure you've been yapping about. You'll get your cut, don't worry."

She heard the faint hum of the outboard motor on the launch that had brought them to the *Touché*. The hum slowly faded. A frightening silence followed.

"M—Miss Bishop? Carrie?" It was Jolly. "Are you all right in there?"

"No, I'm not all right," she called back. "It's hot, stuffy and cramped in here. Why don't you let me out? I'm not going anywhere."

"I would, but the door's locked and Charlie has the key. I'd help you if I could. Charlie has no call to treat you like this. I had no idea. He promised he wouldn't hurt any-one—"

"You *can* help me, Jolly. Get on the radio. Call for help."

"The radio's locked in the bridge. I can't get to it."

Carrie considered her alternatives. "Is there any way for you to get to shore from here?" she asked.

There was a pause before Jolly answered. "I can swim. It's a long way, but I've done it before."

"Good, that's good." Then what would he do, Carrie wondered. Go to the police? She shuddered as she pictured the boy telling his story to the skeptical Detective Van Horn. Jack! Jack would know what to do. But would Jolly be able to find him before Charlie did?

"When you get to shore, go to my hotel and ask for a woman named Myra. She works in the lobby. Tell her what's happened, and ask her to help you find Jack."

"Yes, Ma'am. I'll find Jack, that's what I'll do."

Jack stared through his mask in frozen fascination. With one swipe of his paddle he had uncovered a carpet of gold coins, more gold than he'd ever seen in one place at one time. It was only an hour ago that he had persuaded Gifford to spend one more stint guarding his boat while he dived at the *Laurel* site. He had returned to the place where Carrie discovered the dagger, hoping against hope the area would be hot. And it was.

He picked up one of the doubloons and checked the date: 1749. Each coin he examined was mint-fresh, bearing the same year. The doubloons didn't bring him any closer to identifying the wreck, but when such a quantity of coins was brought to light, the university could hardly deny that Jack had found *something* significant. Would it be enough?

He took several photos of the coins just as he'd uncovered them, made some measurements, jotted down a few notes on his slate. Then gingerly he picked up the coins one by one, twenty-seven in all, and dropped them in his goody bag.

He went to work with the paddle again, moving the sand around little by little. A large outcropping of coral close by could be hiding a multitude of artifacts. Unfortunately he didn't have the right tools with him to tackle the hard, sharp growths. It was frustrating not to be able to do a proper survey.

More than an hour passed, but Jack found nothing more. He checked his air supply. Another five minutes before he needed to head back. There was time for one more pass with the paddle.

He thought he saw something, a brief sparkle. Then he heard a noise, and the sparkle was momentarily forgotten. A boat was approaching. He looked toward the *Carrie*, anchored a hundred yards away, but saw nothing.

He'd better head back. Jack had dug out his pistol for Gifford to keep with him—just in case—but the old man was not necessarily safe just because he had a gun.

Jack spared one backward look at the place where he thought he'd seen the sparkle. Somehow, miraculously, the sands had shifted when he'd had his back turned. Now, lying on top of the sand as if someone had just dropped it there, was a gold sea horse with rubies for eyes and a large diamond in its coiled tail.

Jack grabbed onto it before it could slip away again. But there was no time for close scrutiny now. The boat he'd heard was drawing closer. Mentally he marked the spot where he'd found the sea horse, shoved the beautiful artifact into his bag and began strong, measured strokes toward his boat.

Another boat had pulled up next to the *Carrie*, Jack noted as he drew closer. He surfaced quietly and had a look around. He didn't recognize the visiting craft.

Gifford's voice, unusually agitated, floated through the air. "Jack should be returning to the surface any minute. He will know what to do."

Jack's every muscle tensed as he removed his fins and threw them on deck before grasping the ladder to climb aboard himself.

"Thank heavens you are here, my friend," Gifford said as he assisted Jack onto the boat. "Come, we have no time. Miss Carrie is in trouble."

Jack sprang into action, fear and dread and adrenaline causing him to move quickly, efficiently. "What kind of trouble?" he demanded as he hauled up the anchor.

Gifford started the motor. "I will explain on the way. But we must hurry."

The driver of the other boat called to him. "This way, follow me!" As both boats sprang into motion, Jack realized the driver was none other than Jolly Roger.

"The boy has defected to our side," Gifford explained a few minutes later. "Now that he's seen what real pirates do, he's no longer interested in being one. He wants to help Carrie, and I feel we should trust him."

Jack grumbled in reply. He didn't like putting his trust in a double-crossing kid, not when Carrie's life was at risk. But at the moment, he had little choice.

Carrie shifted her weight once again, trying to find a position in the stuffy, cramped closet that would afford her some slight comfort. How long had it been? Two hours? Three? She had no sense of time in the constant darkness.

However long she'd been there, she'd had plenty of time to think. What else was there to do? She'd forced herself to think about her confrontation with Jack at the library, reliving every word they'd spoken to each other in excruciating detail. Had she misread his reaction? Had she been wrong to run away from him?

He'd said he wanted her on the plane to the States. That seemed to pretty well clarify Jack's feelings about her. But maybe he was simply scared of commitment. Lots of men were. Perhaps if she assured him that she had no intention of tying him down... *Oh, baloney, Carrie Bishop, you're deluding yourself.*

She forced herself to think of something else, to get her mind off Jack and the subtle rocking of the boat that threatened to make her nauseous, on top of everything else.

She'd think about Christmas. It was only a few days away. When all this was over, maybe she'd go home after all and spend the holidays with her family. But no, she had to abandon that line of thinking. St. Thomas was her home now, regardless of everything that had happened. Maybe next year she could fly to Iowa for a visit. . . .

It occurred to her then that there might not be a next year for her. Charlie Hill wasn't playing a parlor game here. People who carried guns usually knew how to shoot them, and once he got the information about the *Laurel* from Jack he wouldn't have much use for her.

Her thoughts progressed in a natural circle to Jack. Would she ever see him again? She ached to have him hold her, even if it was for a short time. She longed to tell him all the things that were in her heart, the feelings she'd held closely guarded, even from herself. She loved him. If she never did anything else, she wanted to tell him that. It might not make any difference to him, but the words needed to be said.

She heard a noise. Oh, please, let it be Jack come to rescue me, she thought fervently. But it was Charlie returning. And from the way he was banging things around and barking orders to his second-in-command, his mission to find Jack and pry information out of him hadn't met with success. Good.

She heard a key in the lock, felt the whoosh of fresh air as the closet door opened. Bright rays of light from the setting sun hurt her eyes, but the tangy sea air was a blessing to her lungs. She took in a couple of grateful breaths as Charlie hauled her to her feet.

"Where's Jolly?" he rasped at her as he led her to the sofa.

Carrie shrugged, sinking down into the soft upholstery. Her sharp eyes noted the absence of the gun, but she had no doubt the weapon was close by. If only she could get her hands on it! "I have no idea what happened to the boy," she answered. "I thought he was supposed to keep an eye on me, not the other way around."

Charlie didn't seem overly concerned about Jolly's absence. "Jack wasn't at the library," he said. "In fact, he wasn't at his lab, either, or at his home. And Myra said he hadn't been seen at the hotel all day."

Bless you, Myra, for lying, Carrie thought, knowing full well Myra was the first person Jack had talked to when he entered the lobby.

"That leaves only one place." Charlie turned to Ramon. "Pull up anchor and set sail for St. John."

Ramon left silently to do his captain's bidding.

Carrie had a strong premonition that Charlie was right. The wreck site was a logical place for Jack to go, especially now that he found himself unencumbered by a troublesome female. After all, treasure hunting was his first, probably his only, love, and he was always anxious to return to it. The crucial question was, who would find him first, Jolly or Charlie?

The yacht's motor rumbled to life. She couldn't just sit there and let Charlie sneak up on Jack. She had to *do* something! A plan came to her then, something she'd already unconsciously laid the groundwork for. If the idea repulsed her, well, she'd just have to grit her teeth and go through with it, anyway.

Charlie had sat his bulk down on one of the immovable bar stools to pour himself a Scotch. His immediate attention was not on her.

Though her hands were still tied, she retained some mobility. She undid the top button of her pink cotton blouse and pushed the collar open a bit.

"Say, um, Mr. Hill?" she tried experimentally.

He looked up at her, clearly irritated.

She stood and attempted a seductive walk toward him. "A couple of hours in a hot closet sure can make a girl thirsty. Would you mind pouring me one of those?"

"Sure, why not?" He reached up to a shelf behind the bar and pulled down a glass. "You take it straight up?"

She nodded and took the seat next to his. "You know," she continued as he poured out half a glass of the amber liquid, "I had a lot of time to think while you were gone and, um, it occurred to me that my loyalties are slightly misplaced."

"Oh?" Charlie eyed her skeptically.

"Something you said earlier got me to thinking about it. I mean, Jack did dump me. Why should I protect his stupid treasure when I'm not going to benefit from it? Anyway, you seem to have the odds in your favor. You've already taken one treasure away from Jack, and I suspect you can do it again. You're a very powerful man, Charlie. I like that. I find it extremely sexy."

Carrie took a long sip of her drink to keep herself from groaning aloud at her own B-movie performance. The whiskey burned all the way down to her stomach, bringing tears to her eyes. How could she possibly expect Charlie to fall for this?

But he was grabbing the bait—she could tell by the way he leered at her. He was just egotistical enough to believe that she found him desirable. His eyes nearly popped out of his head as he looked her over from head to toe, feasting on the cleavage her open shirt revealed. He licked his lips. "So you admit there is a treasure?" he asked.

"Uh-huh. There's a sunken pirate ship called the, um, *Flying Dolphin*," she improvised, borrowing a name she'd run across during her research. "And the reason you never find anything when you dive is you aren't looking in the right place. Jack knew someone was watching him all along, so he always anchored the boat several yards away from the real hot spot."

"Exactly how many yards, and in which direction?" Charlie asked, his voice deceptively quiet.

Carrie favored him with a smoldering stare as she took another sip of Scotch. The taste wasn't too bad, now that she was getting used to it. "Oh, I never really measured the distance or looked at a compass. But I imagine I could find the spot for you—for a price."

"Huh. What kind of price did you have in mind? You know, I might still shoot you and throw you overboard for fish food," he said sourly. Then his expression contorted into something downright sinister. "But I might reconsider—for a price of my own." He reached one chubby hand toward her, touched his index finger to her cheek.

She forced herself not to flinch, and instead gave a low whistle of appreciation. "You're no pushover, are you?" She cocked one eyebrow at him, slid off her bar stool and leaned close to him. She could smell his breath, his stifling cologne, his sweat, and she struggled not to shy away in revulsion. "What price did you have in mind?" she whispered.

Her come-on had the desired effect. Charlie put his arms around her. "Well, well. Isn't this a pleasant change of pace?"

Smiling, Carrie tried to loop her arms over his head. But with her wrists tied together, the result was awkward at best. She cleared her throat and looked expectantly at Charlie.

"All right, all right," he said, producing a pocketknife to cut her ropes. She tried not to laugh with relief. Her ploy was working much better than she could have dreamed, but the real test was yet to come.

When her hands were free, she smiled gratefully and eased her arms around Charlie's neck, mentally cringing against the kiss she knew was coming.

"Yes, I think we can negotiate a price we'll both enjoy," Charlie murmured, just before his rubbery lips claimed hers.

She shuddered in disgust, hoping he saw it as a shiver of delight. As the kiss dragged out for interminable seconds, her hands searched behind him for the object she knew was there. Yes, that was it. Her fingers closed around the neck of the Scotch bottle. She had to act now, before she lost the opportunity. She brought the bottle backward and smashed it with all her strength over Charlie's head.

He sighed and went suddenly limp. Carrie stumbled back and wiped her mouth with the back of her hand. She swiped at a tickling sensation on her forehead—blood. She felt dizzy and realized some of the bottle glass must have cut her. But there was no time to worry about that now.

Quickly she disengaged herself from Charlie. He sat slumped on the stool, appearing to be blissfully asleep.

Don't wake up yet, she pleaded silently, using the ropes Charlie had just cut to tie his hands to the back of the bar stool. Her fingers were clumsy, and the growing darkness didn't help, but she didn't want to waste time looking for the light switch.

When she was sure Charlie was secure, she turned her attention toward her next threat, the man in the bridge. She searched Charlie's pockets until she found two things: the keys to the utility closet and the gun.

With the gun in her hand, she crept up a flight of stairs in what she guessed was the direction of the bridge. She felt ridiculous, like a little girl playing Nancy Drew, as she peeked through doors and around corners, searching for Ramon while trying not to be spotted. She wasn't sure she could actually make herself fire the gun, but if she was lucky, she wouldn't have to.

She found Ramon at the helm, feet propped up, an unlit cigar clamped in his teeth as he perused a raunchy magazine.

She opened the door wide. "Freeze, sucker!" she shouted in her best imitation of a TV cop. "Hands in the air."

Ramon took one look at the gun and did as she commanded, no questions asked.

It was amazing the respect one deadly little piece of metal could get, Carrie thought idly. "Lead the way down to the salon," she ordered.

He obeyed without a fuss, even when she told him to get in the utility closet. When she was satisfied that the door was securely locked, she breathed a sigh of relief—until she realized that the yacht was heading full speed toward shore with no one at the helm.

By the time Carrie had scurried up two flights of stairs to the bridge, the coast of St. John was looming distressingly close. She grabbed the wheel and spun it around. Reefs and rocks seemed to be everywhere, surrounding her in the growing twilight. Any second now she expected to hit one, to feel the sickening lurch of the boat. How could she make the boat stop?

Think, Carrie, don't go hysterical now. There was the throttle, right in front of her face. High. Low. Neutral. The boat slowed. Carrie breathed deeply. She was going to survive. No, she was going to pass out.... She slid to the floor and put her head between her knees.

Jack was the first one to spot the *Touché*, circling erratically near the western tip of St. John. By the time he reached it, however, the yacht had slowed and was drifting aimlessly, its motor idling. He sounded his horn. There was no answering signal, no sign of life.

"Get on the radio," he told Gifford. "Tell the Coast Guard where we are." By that time Jolly's boat had caught up with Jack's. "How many people on board?" Jack asked the boy.

"Just three, counting Carrie," he called back. "Hold on, I'm coming with you."

"You stay put. I may have enough trouble as it is." He eyed his gun distastefully before shoving it into the waistband of his shorts. Gifford nosed the *Carrie* up to the back of the *Touché*. Jack grabbed on to the ladder and climbed up on deck.

All was quiet and dark. He entered the first door he came to, and found himself in a large room of some kind. Reflexively, he reached for a light switch. When he flipped it up, he was momentarily taken aback by what he saw. A man was tied to a bar stool, unconscious. Upon closer inspection, Jack was further shocked. It was his old nemesis Charlie Hill—older, *fatter*, but Charlie none the less.

"Well, I'll be damned," he said aloud. That explained a lot of things.

A loud banging claimed Jack's attention. "Hey, is somebody out there? Let me out!"

With his gun drawn, Jack tried the closet door from which the cries originated. "It's locked," he said. "Tell me where to find Carrie Bishop, and I'll try and locate a key."

"Last I saw her she was waving a gun in my face and stuffing me in here. She's one mean mama."

Carrie? A mean mama?

"Try the bridge," the anonymous man suggested. "Someone must be up there. We haven't wrecked yet."

Jack took the man's suggestion and headed upstairs. When he found the bridge, he flinched at what he saw: Carrie, sprawled on the floor, a trickle of blood down her forehead and a gun lying beside her.

Chapter Ten

Jack went to her, dropped to his knees beside her and was relieved to find that her pulse beat strongly. He chafed her hands, then patted her face. "Carrie, honey, c'mon, wake up."

Her eyes fluttered open. "Jack? Oh, Jack, it is you!"

"Lord, Carrie, I thought you were dead. You're bleeding, and—"

"It's not bad," she assured him, unconsciously reaching up to feel the small cut on her forehead. "And it's self-inflicted, at that."

"Are you sure you're not hurt?"

"I don't think so. I just fainted, that's all."

Jack let the relief wash over him. He wanted to take her in his arms, hold her, kiss away the pain and bewilderment he saw in her eyes. Instead he took her hand and squeezed it. "Just the same, don't try to sit up yet."

"All right. Oh, Jack, do something about the boat. It's drifting, we've got to anchor it. The rocks—"

Reluctantly Jack left her to search the bridge. He found the switch that lowered the anchor and put it to use. "There, that should secure us." He immediately returned to her side.

"And we've got to call the police," she said. "I left two men downstairs—"

"Don't worry, the Coast Guard is on its way. And yes, I found your victims. Nice job, Ma Barker."

Carrie laughed despite her aching head. "You saw Charlie, then?" she asked, pushing herself into a sitting position.

"Yup. Charlie and Claude, they're one and the same, right?"

She nodded.

"Clever. He always was a clever bas—"

"Hey!" a voice called. "Anyone up here?"

Jack tensed, then relaxed when he saw the white uniform pass by the open door. He hadn't heard the Coast Guard boat's approach over the engines of the *Touché*, which were still idling. "In here," he called back.

The office entered the bridge, then halted when he saw Carrie. "Are you hurt, Miss?"

"Not seriously, just shook up a little," Carrie answered.

"This is more complicated than I thought," the officer said, bending to pick up the forgotten gun. "I think we'd better all go downstairs and straighten this out."

Jack remembered his own weapon, which appeared as an obvious bulge in the waistband of his shorts. Rather than cause a misunderstanding, he reached for it with one finger, then handed it to the other man, who nodded appreciatively.

"Since when do you pack a gun?" Carrie asked as they walked down the two flights of stairs. She leaned heavily against him, savoring the security and strength of his supporting arm.

"Since I had something important to protect—you."

She liked the way he said that, and she wondered what he meant by it.

Pandemonium reigned as they entered the salon. Three other members of the Coast Guard were attempting to extract a coherent story from a sputtering Charlie Hill and his cohort, Ramon. Gifford and Jolly were there, also, putting in their two cents' worth in response to Charlie's outrageous lies.

"There she is!" Charlie yelled when he saw Carrie, his French accent firmly in place. "She is the one who tried to hijack my boat. And those two—" he pointed to Gifford and Jack "—are her accomplices."

"He kidnapped me at gunpoint!" Carrie contradicted, alarmed at this turn of events. Wasn't this the part where Charlie was supposed to confess to everything?

"Then how come I'm the one who got hit over the head and trussed up like a turkey?" Charlie shot back.

The accusations flew back and forth, and the men in white uniforms apparently didn't know whom to believe. Finally the captain stood on a chair and gave a sharp whistle. "All right, everybody, let's have some quiet!" He waited until the room fell silent. "Thank you. I'm sure you all have your own story to tell, and you'll get your chance to say your piece. But we'll wait until the Charlotte Amalie police get here. Detective Van Horn seems to think he can shed some light on this matter."

Jack groaned. "We'll spend the rest of our lives in jail if Van Horn gets mixed up in this," he whispered in Carrie's ear as he guided her to the sofa. "And you'd better sit down before you fall down. You look terrible."

"Thanks." She had no doubt she looked a fright. But did Jack have to point out the fact? Hadn't her ego taken enough of a beating today? Just the same, she sank into the sofa gratefully.

He smoothed her hair away from her face in a tender gesture. "You sure you're okay?" he asked, sitting next to her. He ran a light caress down the inside of her arm.

Though she would have thought she was past responding, a delicious shiver worked its way through her body as his touch performed its magic on her. His fingers paused at the angry red marks around her wrist where the rope had burned her skin.

He stiffened with anger. "What the hell did that man do to you?"

"Nothing so awful," she reassured him. "I'm fine, really." The worst part of her ordeal, she realized, was that revolting kiss she'd endured from Charlie. But there was no need to tell anyone about that, ever. Once she took a long, hot shower and got rid of the smell of Scotch and stale cologne, she would dismiss it from her mind.

By the time Van Horn arrived, with half the police force in tow, the tension in the salon was strong enough to taste. He introduced himself in a pompous voice as his eyes scanned the room, eventually coming to rest on Jack.

"Ah, Harrington, of course. I should have known." He turned to one of the Coast Guard officers. "I've waited a long time to pin something on him."

Jack jumped out of his seat. "You might at least listen to the facts before you assume—" He cut himself off when he realized Van Horn was laughing.

"Take it easy, Jack. I said I *wanted* to pin something on you. I didn't say I would." He addressed the room in general. "It just so happens that I checked up on Mr. Claude Colline, alias Charlie Hill, after a complaint was lodged against him several days ago. The man is wanted by the Feds and at least half a dozen states, on charges ranging from speeding to tax fraud to extortion.'' He paused dramatically as a reaction rippled through the room. ''So I'm not inclined to believe he's blameless in today's incident.''

The tension eased itself out of Carrie's muscles one by one. She and Jack weren't going to jail after all. Despite Van Horn's skepticism, he had actually taken their complaint seriously, and had done a creditable job of investigation.

After the detective's enlightening speech, untangling the day's events became a simpler task. Charlie refused to talk until he had a lawyer. Ramon, seeing how the tide was turning, decided to abandon his boss and corroborate Carrie's story, much to her relief. When all statements were taken, Charlie and his partner were fitted with life jackets, handcuffed and taken away by the police.

Jack, with what Carrie surmised was a painful swallowing of pride, offered his hand to Van Horn. ''I'm indebted to you this time, Clive.''

''Perhaps it's the other way around,'' Van Horn replied. ''Charlie Hill is the biggest fish I've ever caught. I might even get a commendation out of—hold it, where's that kid?''

Jack shrugged, then turned to Gifford. ''Do you know what happened to Jolly?''

''I believe he had to return something he borrowed from the hotel,'' Gifford answered, nonchalantly looking up at the ceiling.

Jack and Carrie both nodded their understanding. Jolly had apparently stolen a boat, and had slipped away in the confusion to return it before it was missed. The kid was destined to be a pirate yet.

The Coast Guard took charge of the yacht, leaving Carrie with no alternative but to accept a ride to St. Thomas with Jack and Gifford. Soon she found herself seated on the

Carrie's familiar deck, watching with a strange sort of detachment as the two men went through the routine motions of getting the boat underway.

Now that all the excitement was over, she felt numb and lifeless, at odds with the whole world. A few hours ago she had longed for the opportunity to tell Jack that she loved him. But now that the chance would be hers, she wasn't so sure. How could she find the words to communicate her feelings for Jack, especially in her currently disheveled, stressed state? Would she be able to sit still and listen as he tried to explain his reasons for rejecting her?

Her thoughts were muddled, and her head throbbed. Perhaps a hot shower was what she needed after all. There was a small bathroom—*head*, she corrected herself—below. No one would miss her if she slipped away for five minutes.

Unobserved, she made her way to the captain's quarters and stripped off her stale clothes. She gasped as she caught sight of her image in the mirror, with dried blood smeared over her face and matted into her hair. No wonder Jack had feared she was dead.

With a grimace she turned away from the mirror and entered the tiny shower stall in the adjoining bathroom. She let the small stream of warm water cascade over her with a sigh of relief, then soaped and lathered and shampooed and rinsed until she was sure not a trace of the day's debacle remained on her person.

Even after she was clean, she let the stream of warm water wash over her for an extra minute or so. She felt safe and relaxed for the first time in days. If only she could crawl directly into a warm bed and avoid talking to Jack altogether, at least until morning. She didn't suppose that was possible.

As she emerged from the shower, she noticed that the boat was now merely idling. Had they already reached the hotel?

She quickly dried off, then realized she didn't have a scrap of fresh clothing to put on. And her suitcases were still in the trunk of Charlie's car! She'd just have to borrow something of Jack's.

Feeling like a thief, she plundered dresser drawers until she found an old pair of shorts, a frayed cloth belt and a faded T-shirt. As she dressed, the boat lurched and started moving once again. Jack must have stopped for gas, she decided.

When Carrie made her way on deck, she instinctively sought out the familiar, comforting silhouette of Gifford. He was nowhere to be seen. Not only that, the lights of St. Thomas were receding behind the boat.

Carrie stormed up to the bridge. She was in no mood for Jack's high-handedness. "Jack Harrington! Where are we going?" she demanded, having forgotten all her tender thoughts of minutes before.

Jack didn't appear the least riled by her inquisition. He sat in the captain's chair, ankles crossed negligently, one hand on the wheel. "Something wrong?"

"You know darn well something's wrong. We're supposed to be over there!" She pointed to the faraway lights of St. Thomas. "What are we doing out here? And where's Gifford?"

Jack eased the throttle to neutral and cut the engine. It was suddenly quiet, with only the sound of waves lapping against the side of the boat. "I dropped Gifford off at the marina to pick up his cab. And we're out here because it was the only place I could think of where you can't run away from me. I have a few things to say to you."

"I thought you stated your case pretty clearly at the library," she said coolly.

"I stated my case very poorly," he corrected her as he stood and took her hand. "Come on, let's go out on deck where we can feel the breeze and see the stars."

Carrie followed his lead, though she wasn't certain she wanted to see the stars. The sight of a million jewels in a black velvet sky and the feel of the warm trade wind against her skin would only make her feel romantic, and that wasn't what she needed right now. She needed a dose of calm, practical reasoning.

"You don't have to explain, you know," she said softly when they'd settled into two deck chairs. "I think I know how you feel, and I can guess what you're going to say."

"Is that so?"

Even though it was dark, Carrie knew he was arching a skeptical eyebrow at her. She rushed on, determined to get the words out in the open, get the painful issues over with quickly. "I truly believe you care about me. But I also know you wouldn't have been so free with your feelings if you'd thought I'd try to hook you into a long-term relationship."

"Would you mind if I—"

"Yes, I would. You've kidnapped me—the second time today someone's hauled me out on a boat against my will, mind you—and the least you can do is let me have my say."

Jack threw up his hands. "Fine. Continue, by all means."

She did. "Lots of men are leery of anything that smacks of commitment. You, especially, have good reason to be, given your life-style and all. When I told you I intended to stay on St. Thomas, you had every right to react as you did. I honestly don't blame you. I . . ." She was surprised and dismayed when her eyes suddenly filled with tears, and in the middle of such a sensible speech, too. She was grateful that the darkness hid the moisture that escaped and trick-led down her cheek.

Difficult as it was, she aired the rest of her thoughts. "I love you, Jack, but I know when to let go."

Jack stared at her, dumbfounded. If she loved him, then why had she—how *could* she have gotten everything so cockeyed?

He pushed himself up from the chair and began to pace. "You think you have me all figured out, don't you?" He turned toward her swiftly, pointing an accusing finger. "It just so happens that you're way off base, so far off that I could almost laugh about it if it didn't make me so mad."

Carrie shrank into her chair. She'd never seen him this fired up, at least not when the anger was directed at her. She'd meant to smooth things over, but apparently she'd bungled the job.

"Of course I wanted you on a plane out of here," he continued. "I've been trying to get you off this island al-most since the day we met. But not because I wanted to be rid of you, you little idiot. I wanted you out of harm's way. I dragged you into danger, then proceeded to do a lousy job of protecting you, or hadn't you noticed?"

Carrie lowered her lashes and said nothing.

"I'll admit I lost my head when you told me you were staying here permanently. I didn't want you to leave me...but I sure didn't want to see you dead. And that was a very real possibility. Can't you see that now?"

Carrie swallowed, unable to find the words to respond. She certainly *had* been off base.

"In your defense," he said, lowering his voice, "I didn't express myself very well at the library. In fact, I acted like a barbarian, ordering you to be on that plane without offer-ing any explanation. No wonder you misunderstood. I'm sorry I didn't choose my words more carefully."

"I didn't give you much of a chance to explain," said Carrie in a tiny voice.

Jack settled into the deck chair, his anger spent. He took her hand and rubbed his thumb absently over her knuckles. They sat that way in silence for several minutes. But it was only an intermission. Jack had more to say, and if he didn't get everything off his chest tonight he might not get the chance.

"Are you still planning to catch the first plane home?" he asked. "Myra told me you were headed to the airport this afternoon."

Her answer surprised him. "Actually, no. Despite everything that's happened, I've decided to stick to my original plan. St. Thomas is my home now. But don't worry, I'll keep out from under your feet."

Jack shook his head, chuckling without humor. "You still think I don't want you here."

Carrie sighed. "Truth is, I'm not sure what to think anymore. It's been a confusing day."

"Then let me spell it out for you. I'm pleased you're staying. No, that's understating my case. I'm *ecstatic*. And I don't know where you got this idea that I'm afraid of a long-term relationship. I've just never met a woman who inspired me to make a commitment. At least, not until you came along."

Carrie, who had been avoiding his gaze, now looked directly at him, her eyes wide with astonishment.

His voice gentled. "Yes, you, my dear, have unsettled my life in more ways than one. If you had gone back to Iowa I would have gone after you. I want you to stay with me, always. In fact, I want us to get married. Now, how's that for long-term commitment, huh?"

Carrie reacted with a long, shocked silence. When she finally rediscovered her voice, it came out as a mere squeak. "Did you just say—"

"You heard right. I just proposed marriage. Do you want it on one knee? Standing on my head? I love you, Carrie, though God knows why. You've been a real pain in the rear today."

It wasn't the most romantic proposal in the world, but that didn't bother Carrie. A flower of pure joy was blooming in her heart. Jack loved her and wanted her, and that was all that mattered.

Or was it? Hadn't her first marriage taught her anything?

She held back the affirmative answer she longed to give. "Have you, um, thought this through?" she asked instead.

"What's to think through? We love each other, damn it."

"We're two very different people," she said carefully. "You lead an adventurous, exciting life. Mine is much more tranquil. Oh, sure, I came here looking for a little excitement, but believe me, I've had my fill of the fast life, and I'd just as soon go back to domesticity. I'd be perfectly content if I never again had to face anything more dangerous or exotic than a lizard in the house. Now is that the kind of wife you want?"

"Carrie, you're—"

"Think about it, Jack. What if I turn out to be an anchor around your neck?"

Jack sighed expansively. "You stubborn woman, you'd be no such thing. I'm an archaeologist, not an adventurer—that's *your* label. Do you think this has been a typical week in my life? Most of the time my work is regular and tedious. Nine-to-five stuff. You might be surprised at how tranquil and domestic I can be."

Carrie tried not to let herself be swayed. "The treasure-hunting bug will bite you again," she argued. "You'll hear a rumor and first thing you know you'll be wanting to run off to the Yucatan or the Canary Islands, and here you'll have this wife—"

He cast her a dangerous look that caused her to bite her tongue. She hadn't intended to make him angry again, but she had to be sure he had studied all the angles.

When Jack spoke, his voice was surprisingly soft. "Believe me, Carrie, my wandering days are over. I have no reason to feel bitter or restless anymore. Charlie Hill is going to jail, I've got the *Constantine*, and if you'd just agree to marry me, this will have turned out to be one of the best days of my life."

But Carrie's attention had faltered at the mention of the wreck. "What do you mean, you've got the *Constantine*?"

She could see his smile in the starlight. "I'd forgotten all about it until you mentioned treasure. Come with me, I have something to show you." He led her to the back of the boat, where his equipment was stowed, and she followed eagerly, bursting with curiosity. He opened a storage compartment and pulled out his goody bag.

Carrie could already see the sparkle of gold through the mesh. She gasped as he opened the bag for her inspection. So many gold coins! And something else... She reached into the bag and pulled out the strange object. A gold sea horse, its eyes glittering with rubies, its tail coiled around a huge diamond....

"It's just like on the cargo manifest." She scarcely breathed the words. "You've done it. You've found the proof. You'll get your grant. Oh, Jack!" She couldn't help herself. She threw her arms around his neck and gave him a congratulatory hug. "Why didn't you tell me right away?"

"I had more important things on my mind."

She blushed to think she was more important to him than the glittering prize she held. "Finding the sea horse made this past week worthwhile, didn't it?"

His eyes, smiling down at her only a moment before, grew dark and serious. "Nothing is worthwhile if you're not here to share it with me. So put me out of my misery. Is it yes or no?"

Carrie could sense a stillness in Jack, a seed of contentment that was missing before. She believed he meant what he said—he would settle down.

"Yes," she said in a clear, sure voice. "Yes, I'll marry you." She'd found the real treasure in her life, and she intended to keep it.

Their celebratory kiss was swift and strong, as pure and intense as their emotions. There were no teasing, nipping caresses, there was no laughter, no shyness, just a white-hot current of emotion coursing between them, binding them. Chest to chest, their hearts thudded as one, and their breathing accelerated in unison.

They were the only two people for miles around, but they might as well have been the only two in the world. Jack cradled her head under his chin, stroked her hair and sighed contentedly.

Epilogue

Once the small chartered seaplane was airborne, Carrie leaned her seat back to gaze out the window at the sparkling Caribbean. The sun was so bright and the water so clear, she could see straight to the sandy bottom of the shallows below.

Three days had passed since her ordeal with Charlie Hill, three glorious, breathless days during which Carrie had made feverish plans for a wedding and Jack had made mysterious arrangements for a honeymoon.

She'd thrived on the excitement of launching their marriage. But throughout the frenzied preparations, her imagination had often taken her forward in time to when she and Jack could at last be relaxed—and alone.

Now that time was here. "Tell me about this place where you're taking me," she said to Jack. "Thus far all I've managed to pry out of you is that it's an island called Gorlez. Are you sure there is such a place? I've never heard of it."

"It's one of the smallest inhabited islands in the Caribbean," he explained. "A university regent owns a villa there, which is empty at the moment. We have it all to ourselves for the next week."

Carrie closed her eyes and painted a beautiful mental picture of their private villa. It was just what she would have ordered for the perfect honeymoon. "Mmm, I love it already."

Jack smiled wickedly. "It'll be just you and me and white sand beaches and a fully stocked refrigerator. We'll have nothing to do but eat, sleep, take long walks and be totally bored."

Carrie cleared her throat. "I think you forgot something."

He reached up to caress her cheek, then kissed her for the umpteenth time since they'd exchanged vows only hours earlier. "I haven't forgotten," he murmured, nuzzling her ear. "Not for a minute."

She giggled with delight, then sighed and closed her eyes. "Rest and relaxation, just what we deserve. In fact, after what we've been through, I can't think of anything more appealing than boredom."

"It'll be wonderful," he agreed. "Just one serene day running into another, with nothing more strenuous to do than blink...are you sure you don't mind being bored?"

"Of course not."

Jack wasn't really worried that Carrie would be bored on their honeymoon, but what about the coming months and years when he would be working day after day on the salvage operation?

As if picking up on his thought waves, Carrie asked, "When you're done with the *Constantine*, what next? Will you look for another shipwreck?"

"No, no, I'm done with all that. I don't need to discover anything else. After all, I've got the *Constantine* and a beautiful, sweet, loving wife to share my success with. What more could I want?"

Carrie smiled at his pretty words, but in the back of her mind she wondered if he was trying to convince himself as well as her. Was she already tying him down? But no, she was being silly. She forced herself to take a deep breath and enjoy the incomparable view out the seaplane's window.

"How soon will we get there?" she asked.

"About fifteen more minutes." He leaned sideways so he could peer out the small window alongside her. "That's Gorlez, off to the right just on the horizon."

"Oh, it is tiny. What do you call those little islands right below us?"

Jack directed his attention to the scattering of coral heads that could scarcely be called islands. "Those are just rocks," he answered. "They probably don't even have names...." But his words trailed off as his eyes focused on a strange coral formation in the water below. It looked distinctly unnatural.

"What's wrong? What are you staring at?" Carrie asked.

"Oh, uh, nothing, really. Did you bring some binoculars?"

"Yes, I have them right here." She reached into a tote bag under her seat and withdrew a small pair of field glasses. But she held them just out of Jack's reach. "First tell me what you want them for."

Jack knew she wouldn't let him rest until he told her what had sparked his interest. He pointed out the window. "See those straight lines on the bottom just to the left of the biggest rock?"

"No...oh, yes, I see them now."

He took the field glasses from her and peered through them for several seconds. "It appears to be an old cannon." As the plane took them away from the rocks, Jack pulled back from the window and returned the binoculars to Carrie.

"Cannon. You mean from a shipwreck?" An unexpected shot of adrenaline coursed through Carrie's body. She tried to get a good look through the binoculars at the area in question, but the plane had moved too far away.

"Could be," Jack answered, managing to sound bored. "Or it might just be some old junk used for ballast that a ship threw out when it found itself too close to the rocks."

"Don't you, uh, want to take a closer look?" she asked cautiously.

He settled back into his seat and closed his eyes "Nope. I want to start my honeymoon."

"But, Jack..."

He opened one eye and peered at her suspiciously. "What?"

"Aren't you the least bit curious?"

Now he opened both eyes. "Are you?"

"No," she answered hastily. "No, of course not."

"Good. Because if I remember correctly you were looking forward to some R and R, and discovering a shipwreck is not a restful endeavor—as you well know."

She sighed. "You're right. What would we do with another old shipwreck? Anyway, we don't have the diving gear with us, so there's no point in even discussing it."

There was a long pause before Jack spoke again. "To be honest, I *did* bring along a couple of tanks, just in case we wanted to...look at some coral," he finished weakly.

Carrie chanced a sideways glance at him. He looked guilty as hell. "Nothing more strenuous than blinking, huh? Admit it, Jack, you were planning all along to do some serious diving. And I know you want to go back and take a look at that cannon.''

He shook his head emphatically. "Not me. You're the one who's curious about it. Why don't you just admit that you have an adventurous streak a mile wide?''

"I do not," she insisted. "I'm intrigued, that's all . . . but you're right, it's not important," she added.

Who did she think she was fooling? Jack thought. The woman was consumed with curiosity. "Well, I don't suppose it would hurt anything if we had a quick look at the cannon—since you're curious. We'll stop for thirty minutes, tops. Then it's straight on to Gorlez for some R and R. Agreed?''

Carrie struggled to keep her excited laughter in check. Who did he think he was fooling? "Oh, absolutely. A quick look. Thirty minutes, tops.''

*   *   *   *   *

SILHOUETTE DESIRE™
presents
AUNT EUGENIA'S TREASURES
by CELESTE HAMILTON

Liz, Cassandra and Maggie are the honored recipients of Aunt Eugenia's heirloom jewels...but Eugenia knows the real prizes are the young women themselves. Read about Aunt Eugenia's quest to find them everlasting love. Each book shines on its own, but together, they're priceless!

Available in December:
THE DIAMOND'S SPARKLE (SD #537)

Altruistic Liz Patterson wants nothing to do with Nathan Hollister, but as the fast-lane PR man tells Liz, love is something he's willing to take *very* slowly.

Available in February:
RUBY FIRE (SD #549)

Impulsive Cassandra Martin returns from her travels... ready to rekindle the flame with the man she never forgot, Daniel O'Grady.

Available in April:
THE HIDDEN PEARL (SD #561)

Cautious Maggie O'Grady comes out of her shell...and glows in the precious warmth of love when brazen Jonah Pendleton moves in next door.

Look for these titles wherever Silhouette books are sold, or purchase your copy by sending your name, address and zip or postal code, along with a check or money order for $2.50 for each book ordered, plus 75¢ postage and handling, payable to Silhouette Reader Service to:

In U.S.A.	In Canada
901 Fuhrmann Blvd.	P.O. Box 609
P.O. Box 1396	Fort Erie, Ontario
Buffalo, NY 14269-1396	L2A 5X3

Please specify book title(s) with your order.

Wonderful, luxurious gifts can be yours with proofs-of-purchase from any specially marked "Indulge A Little" Harlequin or Silhouette book with the Offer Certificate properly completed, plus a check or money order (do not send cash) to cover postage and handling payable to Harlequin/Silhouette "Indulge A Little, Give A Lot" Offer. We will send you the specified gift.

Mail-in-Offer

	OFFER CERTIFICATE			
Item	A Collector's Doll	B Soaps in a Basket	C. Potpourri Sachet	D Scented Hangers
# of Proofs-of -Purchase	18	12	6	4
Postage & Handling	$3.25	$2.75	$2.25	$2.00
Check One				

Name _____

Address _____ Apt # _____

City _____ State _____ Zip _____

ONE PROOF OF PURCHASE

To collect your free gift by mail you must include the necessary number of proofs-of-purchase plus postage and handling with offer certificate.

SR-3

Harlequin®/Silhouette®

Mail this certificate, designated number of proofs-of-purchase and check or money order for postage and handling to:

INDULGE A LITTLE
P.O. Box 9055
Buffalo, N.Y. 14269-9055